Tales of Horror
Macabre Monsters of Michigan

Bryan C. Laesch

Copyright © 2017 Bryan C. Laesch
All rights reserved.

No portion of this book may be reproduced in any form without permission from the publisher, except as permitted by U.S. copyright law. For permissions contact: bryanclaesch@yahoo.com.

ISBN: 978-1521889039

Cover designed by Corvid Design

Table of Contents

Acknowledgements v

Re: Encounter 1

The Serpent 24

    Prologue 24

    Day 1 28

    Day 2 41

    Day 3 71

    Day 4 75

    Day 5 78

    Day 6 92

    Epilogue 104

Becoming The Dragon 106

    The Reading 106

    Dark Ascension 120

    Consummation 129

    The Occult Killer 130

Coming Attractions 131

Feature 1 131

Feature 2 136

Author's Afterword 144

About the Author 145

Acknowledgements

Firstly, I would like to acknowledge the hard work and commitment of my beta reader Sarah. Her help and excitement showed me that I really do have something here.

Secondly, I would like to thank my family and friends who believe I actually have a talent for writing and continue to support me in pursuing my dream.

Re: Encounter

To: SuperCuteTXNGirl75

From: LoneShepherdinMI73

Subject: US Pen Pals: Greetings from Michigan!

Date: April 25, 2000

Hi, there! I was matched with you through US Pen Pals. I thought I'd take the initiative and introduce myself.

The name's Rawlin. I'm 27 with brown hair and blue eyes. I'm 6'3", and in better than average shape. For work I keep a small-acreage sheep farm. In my free time I like to hunt and fish, and spend time with my dogs. I live out in BFE Michigan where plenty of strange and *spooky* things happen. There's plenty more to tell, but I think that's enough for now.

So, what do you like to do? What do you look like? Do you have any pets? What do you do for a living?

Hope to hear from you soon!

To: SuperCuteTXNGirl75

From: LoneShepherdinMI73

Subject: RE: RE: US Pen Pals: Greetings

Date: April 29, 2000

Hey, Kelly!

I'm glad you replied. You sound like an authentic country girl to me. I love a country girl with a Southern drawl. I like how tall you are, too—you sound beautiful. And I wouldn't mind exchanging "pics" later on, if I know what they are. Is that some kind of Internet slang?

I haven't met many girls who like to fish. Personally, I prefer bowfishing, but I do like to catch pan fish once in a while. I have my own boats: a canoe for regular fishing and a slightly larger rig for bowfishing. What else do you like to do? Do you hunt, hike, swim, etc?

It's funny you should mention Detroit—I'm actually from there originally. I couldn't stand the city. It was…well, for the sake of brevity, it wasn't my scene, hence why I moved out to the country. It's great! There's so much open land that I forget I have neighbors.

I love that you have two dogs yourself. Of course, I like Rotties. I like most dogs. As for mine, I have a 7 yr old German Shepherd, Lady, and two 5 yr old Border Collies: Apollo and Ziggy. Lady was my first—technically she came with the house.

Yes, I do work the farm myself. The dogs help, but it's still a lot of work. Honestly though, I like it that way. Having been born and bred in the city, I never knew what it was like to work hard. But I really like it. You go to bed every night feeling like you accomplished something and the blisters on your hands and feet are proof of that.

As for what sort of spooky things…well, it isn't unusual to hear things scratching or growling after nightfall, and there's all the eye shine you see when you drive down the road. They may just be coons and possums, but they look downright evil in my high beams! Ha ha! Other than that, there is the occasional wolf's howl or fox yelp, which doesn't really concern me as the entire property is bordered by an electric fence.

Anyway, you said you were still in school; are you still going for your bachelor's or are you a grad student?

Rawlin

To: SuperCuteTXNGirl75

From: LoneShepherdinMI73

Subject: Stuff

Date: May 5, 2000

Kelly,

Sorry it took so long to get back to you. I've been really busy the past few days. One of my lambs got really sick and so I had the vet out here. Unfortunately, it's not looking good for him.

Anyway…

Yes, I did go to college. I majored in veterinary sciences. I took a lot of biology and animal behavioral classes, but I dropped out after my parents died. I never stopped learning on my own, though—can't tell you how many books I have on animals, especially dogs and wolves. Wolves have always been my favorite animal since the first time I went to the zoo. There's a real intelligence behind those eyes. And I find the word "wolf" to be mystic in and of itself.

Anyway, sorry about that heavy stuff. So, you're in the nursing program? I've heard that's a hard career to break into. Good luck to you. But your original degree was in English? How did you go from English to nursing?

I'd love to take you hunting. The sport needs more women. I've hunted game all over the country: Alaska, California, S. Carolina, New York, and even Texas. But I'm best at hunting in my home state. I'm going to assume that as a real country gal you've shot a gun before. What guns have you shot?

No doubt you look good in a bikini, but skinny dipping, huh? If I didn't know any better, I'd say you were flirting with me. Ever go skinny dipping in the Great Lakes?

Rawlin

P.S. Lady was left behind by the guy I bought the farm from. She wasn't traumatized, and already knew how to herd.

To: SuperCuteTXNGirl75

From: LoneShepherdinMI73

Subject: RE: RE: Stuff

Date: May 10, 2000

Dear Kelly,

It's okay, you don't have to be sorry about my parents. I made peace with the whole thing years ago.

Truth be told, we were never that close. They always either seemed too busy for me or just didn't want me around. My father would chase his career, and my mother would chase her weird, post-modern art dreams. As a result, I would go out and explore the city. You might think that was irresponsible since it was Detroit, but the upper crust does live some *very* nice neighborhoods. Very safe.

But as I got older, I started taking trips farther and farther from home. I remember the first time I spent the night out in the "wild". I decided to spend the night in a mini-forest within the city limits. At the time, I was scared as hell. But, after, I felt amazing! I felt free—I'd found my independence and felt like I could do anything! From there, it became my goal to explore and camp out in as many forests as possible, which became quite easy when I turned 16 and my parents gifted me a car—more so out of convenience than as a loving gift. But I didn't care. The world was my oyster and the national parks and woodlands my pearls! Oh, how I loved it.

Anyway, it's good to hear you have so much experience with firearms and bows. Now, I won't have to teach you as much when we go hunting. And, of course, we can go fishing in the Great Lakes. We can do some bowfishing and later some skinny dipping, ha ha ha.

Sincerely,

Rawlin

P.P.S. Uh, you asked about the lamb. Unfortunately, he didn't make it. But the circumstances concerning his death are a little weird. I'm not sure you want to hear about it…

To: SuperCuteTXNGirl75

From: LoneShepherdinMI73

Subject: Weird Creature

Date: May 15, 2000

Dear Kelly,

Well, if you'd really like to know…

A couple of days before I emailed you back, something strange happened around here late one night. I was in the house when I heard this wolf's howl. It was deep and almost sounded like a great moan. I'd never heard anything like it before, and the more I concentrated on it, the more it chilled me. I can't explain why. But when I didn't hear it again or a response, I thought it might have been something else. But then as I sat down to write you, I heard my sheep stampede and several distressed baa's. What could have made them stampede, let alone at night, and make such an awful racket? I was worried, especially after having heard the howl. So, I got a flashlight, grabbed a rifle, and went out to investigate.

As I got closer to the herd, I could tell something happened. Dust was kicked up from the ground, there were sheep tracks all around, and there was a distressed baa coming from the center of the reforming flock.

As I investigated, I found the flock parting around one sheep and its lamb. But when I saw the lamb, its body was mangled. I had never seen anything like it. Something had bitten into the lamb's neck and tore it out. There were also claw marks on its flanks, both around its neck and rump. And as I stood there, spellbound by the grisly scene, something moved from the far left. I had heard some dirt be thrown up, but what actually caught my attention was that all the sheep turned their heads to look in the same direction, which they'll do with predators. I shone my flashlight in that direction, but I didn't see anything. I suddenly felt very uncomfortable and ran back to the house.

In the morning, I called the vet to examine the lamb and see if he could tell what had mangled it. He said that it was definitely a predator and looked like a wolf, which would make sense since wolves are known to rip the throats out of their victims, but the tooth and claw marks were too big. The vet also mentioned that the claw marks were quite peculiar as it looked like something had scooped up the lamb in two hands, one at each end, and then ripped out its throat with its teeth. I couldn't believe that because if it was a wolf, they obviously don't have hands. I also don't believe a wolf is capable of jumping a seven-foot, electrified fence. But...I did see something strange about a week ago that might be the culprit...

I was driving home from a small venture in town. I was the only one on a dirt, country road, and as I gazed out my passenger window, I saw something out of the corner of my eye. I looked forward and saw this peculiar creature cross the road. I have no idea what it was, but it had black fur and a dog-like cadence to its walk, but there was something off about it. Now, while I have no idea how far away I was, so I can't accurately judge its size, but it did look rather large. It was oddly long and I would've guessed at least four feet tall at the shoulder. That's weird and impossible, I know, but it did have a sizeable head with a long muzzle and tall, triangular, erect ears. I didn't see a tail, and I didn't see its eyes, but something about it did send a shiver down my spine. It was long like a cougar, tall like a bear, but looked like a wolf. There was also something strange about its body. Its torso didn't look barrel-shaped like most canine torsos are, but I can't say what shape it actually was.

Anyway, it crossed the road and went straight into the tall grass on the other side, disappearing as quickly as it appeared. I looked for it when I passed by that spot, but it was gone. And when the vet had said there was something strange about the lamb's slaughter, I couldn't help but think about the creature. And there was that howl I heard about 20-30 minutes before the incident.

What could it have been? Would you know? I've never seen a wolf that large in the wild, but with a steady diet, they can weigh close to 200 lbs. But what would it be eating out here? Sure, there are wild deer around, but I wouldn't think there were enough to feed a predator that size. If you have any ideas what it might be, I'd like to hear them.

Until then, this has been Rawlin J. Signing off from Weird Michigan.

To: SuperCuteTXNGirl75

From: LoneShepherdinMI73

Subject: RE: RE: Weird Creature

Date: May 19, 2000

A Sasquatch?! Really now… Be serious. Besides, I've never heard of one of those being down on all fours. And what exactly is a "devil cat"? I've heard of the Ozark Howler/Wampus; is that what you mean?

Like I said, I don't know what it was. I did find some prints not too far from where the flock was that night. They were wolf tracks, but they were gigantic! They were over 8 inches long from claws to pad. That's huge! A big wolf will only have a paw print the size of your hand, so how big could this thing be?! Though, I suppose it is possible that the tracks could've been distorted if the ground was wet or damp. But how could a wolf get onto my property? I checked the fence and it's still intact, and nothing's been digging under it. I did check to see if it was still working, which hurt a little, but it can still definitely conduct an electric current. The only way around it is to jump over, but would a predator really do that? I purposely built it tall to prevent such a thing.

The whole thing is odd…but so long as there are no more instances, I don't really care.

And since you liked it so much, this has been Rawlin J. Signing off from Weird Michigan.

To: SuperCuteTXNGirl75

From: LoneShepherdinMI73

Subject: Surveillance

Date: June 10, 2000

Kel,

I know we were making plans to do something later this summer, but it might be better if you didn't come to Michigan. Some strange shit has happened around here. To be brief, a few more sheep have been culled, and it's always the same kind of attack: throat ripped out and claw marks around the front and hind quarters. A few even have broken legs, which is another puzzle. But what really disturbs me is the fact that whatever's doing this seems to be doing it on purpose. I mean, a predator wouldn't simply rip out a sheep's throat—they'd eat as much as they could, wouldn't they?

I've also spotted more footprints. This time, though, instead of finding one or two here or there, I have found several in a row. For whatever reason, as far as I can tell, they're hind prints because the front prints don't show up real well. But if the disturbed ground is anything to go on, the front prints are larger than the hind ones. I mean, they usually are, but these front prints are double the length of the hind! What sort of creature is this?!

This whole situation has gotten so weird, I've decided to go out and buy some surveillance cameras. I might even try calling Animal Control to see if anyone has reported something strange.

Rawlin

To: SuperCuteTXNGirl75

From: LoneShepherdinMI73

Subject: RE: RE: Surveillance

Date: June 11, 2000

Well, I had an *experience* last night.

While I was out buying the surveillance cameras, this wizened Native American man walked up to me. I was taken completely off guard because he moved with complete silence, and he looked exactly like the Indians in the old cowboy movies, minus the feathered headdress.

He paused before he spoke, saying that I was being haunted by a "wicked trickster". Without me asking, he explained that a trickster is a kind of spirit that uses its great intellect to play tricks on people, except that mine had gone bad. He told me I needed sage, and that if I burned it around my property, the smoke would keep the malevolent spirit at bay. Well, I wasn't sure if I believed him, but I decided it wouldn't hurt to try. So, as I drove home that night, I had both a pile of security cameras and as much sage as I could find. I was feeling pretty good, until I was a few miles from home.

Night had fallen and the weather had cooled to a comfortable temperature, so I had my windows rolled down. Everything felt right with the world, until I came to a four-way stop. As I sat there, I noticed I couldn't hear anything. There were no birds, no insects, and no sound other than the rumble of my truck's engine. As I took off, I suddenly felt chilled and extremely uncomfortable. I quickly rolled up my windows and sped up, which proved to be a bad idea.

In my rush to get home, I was going more than twenty over the limit, which meant I got an eye full of something that if I had been doing the speed limit, I probably wouldn't have seen. As I rounded a corner, I saw this great black mass jump across the road in a single bound. What was that "black mass"? While I wish I could say I don't know, I actually very much do. It was long, had the mass of a brown bear, and had a wolfish head, and this time, I was a lot closer so it looked *much* bigger. I would estimate it was ten feet long or more from front claw to back paw. It also seemed to have a strange hump in its back that I hadn't noticed before. Maybe that's why it looks as big as a bear. But the head and fur were unmistakable—it *was* what I had seen the first time.

I unfortunately didn't get a good look at the front paws, but I know for a fact that it had claws of some kind. They reflected light from my truck's headlights, and this time, I did get to see an eye—it was yellow and seemed to glow. Now, that could have been eye shine from the truck's headlights, but for some reason, I didn't get that impression. I had the feeling the eye had its own source of light. Add to that, I think it had a blood-stained muzzle, so it must have just been feeding. With that thought in mind, I raced home, but then felt immediately silly as I knew that whatever that thing was, if I decided to "challenge" it, it would tear me limb-from-limb. So, when I got home, I simply unloaded my truck as fast as I could, bolted my doors, and kept a couple of rifles company all night.

In the morning, I did as the Native American recommended, and I burned the sage around my property. He hadn't given me any instructions on how to do it, so I put most of it in bundles spaced around the perimeter of my property near the fence and lit them on fire. I know they're supposed to burn like incense, so I did blow out the fires and let them smoke. I also kept a bundle of burning sage with me as I moved from place to place to set up the new cameras. I didn't see or hear anything all day, and there hadn't been any losses from the night before, but I did feel super creeped out all day as if something was watching me. And I must say, the sight of several dozen piles of smoking sage make the farm look otherworldly and discomforting, as if I'm trying to keep a demon away or something. Well, we'll see how this turns out.

Rawlin

To: SuperCuteTXNGirl75

From: LoneShepherdinMI73

Subject: (No Subject)

Date: June 13, 2000

Kelly,

I know I haven't given you a chance to respond to my last email, but I need to tell someone this, and I don't have anyone else to turn to.

So, last night I had a very chilling experience. If you read my last email, you'll recall that I compared the sight of the burning sage bundles to something otherworldly, burning incense to ward off a demon. Well, whatever my demon is, sage doesn't seem to have an affect on it…

Nothing happened that first day and so I thought the sage might have worked. But later that night, I was woken out of a dead sleep by a low, guttural howl. It was loud, so I assumed it was close. My dogs must have come to the same conclusion because I could hear them cowering under the bed and whimpering. I debated with myself whether or not I should get up and grab a gun and go outside to defend my flock, but then I remembered the size of the creature as it bound across the road and the size of its claws. Instead, I pulled the bed covers up as if I was frightened child hiding.

Nothing happened for what felt like minutes and I thought it might have left, but then I heard something outside. There was a rhythm to it like someone beating a drum softly, and I realized that as it got closer, I was hearing footsteps. Something either very large or very heavy was walking past my house. The footsteps got closer and closer until they were right outside my bedroom window where they stopped. My heart raced in anticipation of what would happen next when suddenly there was a scratching sound on the side of my house. It would scratch in rhythms of two. *Scratch, scratch*, pause. *Scratch, scratch*, pause. This went on until I thought I was going to go insane. Right before I could scream "Stop it!", it stopped. But then things became weirder.

After a brief pause, the scratching continued, but this time it was on the window, and what's more, it came from a spot on the window well above my head when I stand up. How could that have been?! I was so stumped by the drastic change in height, that I forgot my fear for a second. I thought for sure it was a tree branch or something similar until I remembered there are no trees outside my bedroom. This realization was exclaimed by a sudden, deep, and raspy exhale from outside my window, and again, from well above my head.

I gripped my covers tightly and stared at the window. I couldn't see what it was that made the noises due to my pulled shades, but I had a terrible sensation of what it was.

As I stared, the footsteps started again, walking away from my bedroom down to the other end of the house. I considered getting up and grabbing a gun. I considered going after it, but I wasn't sure I had anything big enough to intimidate or even kill such a creature. But when my reason started to reclaim me—that it was just an animal—I heard a strange whooshing sound followed by a loud thud as something hit my roof. And then to my great chagrin, the footsteps started again and they came from the roof. They crept closer and closer until whatever it was stopped right above my bedroom. There was a pause followed by a mind-numbing, bladder-emptying, scream-inducing howl! It was the loudest, most terrifying noise I've ever heard. It shook me to my very core as if my primordial being was coming in contact with that which it feared most and had blissfully forgotten. The fear reached such a crescendo alongside the howl that I fainted.

I don't know how long I was out for, but I do remember waking with a shudder and feeling as if I had narrowly escaped death. I think what shook me out of my phobostasis was that all three of my dogs had defecated on the floor and the overbearing stench had gotten to me. I didn't want to get out of bed, but I knew that if I stayed I would end up puking in my sheets.

In the morning, I was skittish about going outside, but I had to. I went loaded for bear and took my dogs with me, although when I rounded the house to the front, they stopped instantly and would go no further. I walked over to my bedroom window and examined the ground. There were a few prints, but they were light. The ground on this side of the house had been baked in the hot summer sun the entire day before. However, what really sent a chill down my spine were the scratches in my house's paint and the just barely visible scratch in my window. I measured the height—it was over seven feet high. With a numb mind, I went back inside and tried to keep my imagination from running away, but it was difficult. I tried to stay busy by checking my security cameras—I don't know why—I didn't want to see the creature—but mercifully they were all blank, but I still searched through them rapidly to avoid the conclusion my brain was struggling to make me see.

I think I'm going to have to call somebody, but I don't know whom.

R.

To: SuperCuteTXNGirl75

From: LoneShepherdinMI73

Subject: Encounter

Date: June 25, 2000

You're gonna think I'm crazy, but I had an experience like no other the other night.

After taking care of my daily duties, I was looking for a way to prevent any more sheep from being killed—yes, you read that right. I'm still having an issue with my sheep getting their throats ripped out and their bodies left behind. Anyway, I had just begun looking over my property, thinking that a few more security lights might do it, when all three of my dogs became very agitated. I've never heard them bark and growl like that before. They eventually stopped and started snarling. They were crouched low with muzzles wrinkled, hackles raised, tails stiffened, and their ears were pinned back. I scanned the flock and saw that their attention was to my far right. I looked and saw a figure approach the fence, bounding on all fours. I couldn't believe I was actually seeing the creature. I've only ever had brief glimpses, but here it was in its full terrible glory! And I watched as it leapt over the electric fence in one go and landed almost silently!

When it landed, my dogs began to whimper and slink away. The creature took notice of us and I could clearly see its shining yellow eyes—they sent a chill down my spine. The creature started to creep in our direction, causing my dogs to run. When I saw them go, I ran back to the house myself. I heard a strange thumping noise and panting behind me. I turned to look and saw the creature chasing after us! It was so damn fast, there was no way we would all make it back to the house. Someone would be caught—probably me!

My dogs beat me back to the house and clawed at the back door till I opened it. I stumbled up the stairs into my kitchen after them, and rather than get up, I rolled onto my back and shut the door with my feet. I quickly locked it with my toe and held it closed with my feet just as I heard something heavy slide to a stop just outside. There was an audible snarl, but nothing else, so I thought we were safe for the moment.

I heard footsteps heading away and I slowly backed away from the door. I slid around my kitchen sink and up to the back window. I slowly peered over the sill. Almost as if it knew what I was doing, the creature walked right into my line of sight. I got a good look at it. It was as I had seen before, but what struck me most was how bulky it was. Despite the thick, coarse fur it had, its musculature was clear, like that of a bodybuilder. What also amazed me were its front paws. Like I had mentioned earlier, they were unusually long, but their dimensions were weird. They weren't thick and rounded like a dog's paw, but rather slender and flat. I moved closer to the window when the creature's head shot up and looked at me with those yellow eyes. Then…it did something I still refuse to believe…

It leaned forward onto its front paws and then rolled its weight back, and started to raise its upper body. My mouth dropped as I saw this thing go from four legs to two! As it neared its full height, there was a strange popping noise from either side of its hips along with a weird contraction. That would make sense since dogs and wolves aren't meant to stand on their hind legs, but this thing did! It stood up straight like a human on its two backward-bent legs. It flexed its front legs and I realized they were arms! And as my eyes neared its paws, it flexed its individual digits and it suddenly made sense that I was looking at hands with four fingers and an opposable thumb. It then pushed out its chest and I was shocked to see the bodybuilder's musculature once again. Its pectorals were large and its abs well defined despite all the fur. It was the most impressive and terrifying thing I've ever seen!

The creature extended its hand out toward me and let out a blood-curdling roar, showing off its reddish-tinted fangs. I wanted to duck behind my counters, but the fact that I was staring at what could only be called a werewolf, morbid curiosity got the better of me. I couldn't stop staring at it despite the fear gripping my heart.

The creature suddenly turned away from me and ran at the flock on its two hind legs. The sheep tried to run, but it easily caught one with its long, strong arms. It grabbed onto a sheep's rear, pulled it back, placed its other hand around its front, and lifted the sheep off the ground. The creature turned to look at me over its shoulder and adjusted almost as if it wanted to show me what it was about to do. It lifted the distressed sheep up and wrapped its jaws around its throat before tearing it out in one motion. It dropped the dying sheep, thus explaining the broken legs, before looking back over its shoulder at me and running down another one.

I slipped behind the sink and sat on the floor. A real monster was just outside my home, killing my flock! It couldn't be real. I hoped that I would wake up any minute, that it was all just some sort of terrible dream.

I could hear my flock stampede every few seconds as the creature tore out their throats one-by-one. Realizing that it was killing my sheep—killing my livelihood—I had to do something. I ran to my gun cabinet and took out the most powerful rifle I had: an M1 Garand. I grabbed a box of .30-06 and ran back to my kitchen. I loaded a clip and shoved it into the gun's magazine. I went to the backdoor and I spotted the creature still wreaking havoc. I was about to grab the door handle when it paused and looked at me through the backdoor window. I stopped. I couldn't go *outside* and shoot it. It was gigantic! It would tear me limb from limb if it got a hold of me.

I went to my kitchen window instead and opened it. I steadied the Garand on the sill and took aim. The creature's frame was several times bigger than my sights—there was no way I could miss, and yet, after I pulled the trigger, the creature merely flinched. I looked over my gun and my mouth dropped. There wasn't any blood, and the creature didn't run. That's when I thought of silver bullets. I almost laughed, because although it looked like a werewolf, I didn't think it was a real one, but I didn't see the harm in trying. I ran to my silverware and took out a fork. I stuck its handle down into the Garand's mag and rubbed the bullet tips with it. I threw the fork in the sink, closed the chamber, and fired the last seven rounds in quick succession.

The creature took off running. First on two legs, but then it dropped down to four right before leaping over my fence in a single bound. I reloaded my gun and went outside to assess the damage. My dogs wouldn't come with me—they were the smarter ones. Sheep bodies lay strewn across the property. There were a dozen or more. The rest of the flock fled to the far side of the enclosure and seemed thoroughly disturbed. I couldn't blame them. I was terribly shaken myself and more so when I got to the spot where the creature was standing. I followed its trail, but there was no blood on the ground. Maybe the rounds embedded themselves into its body, but there still should've been blood somewhere!

Without anything else to do, I cleaned up the sheep bodies and made a few phone calls. I decided my sheep were no longer safe with me and that I should sell them, but I'm sure you know that selling a whole flock, even if greatly depleted, isn't easy. I want to try to sell the farm as I don't really have enough money to move, but selling a farm and a house overnight is no easy task either. Though, if the last guy who owned this property knew about the creature before me, that would explain why he sold it for cheap, but why am I only seeing the creature now?

To be honest, I'm scared. Really scared. You said you were religious, right? I never have been, but there are no atheists in foxholes. I'm ready to start believing in some of that good stuff, now. So, will you pray for me? I could use the help, and I don't know who else to turn to. So, I may need some otherworldly help.

R.

P.S. It means a lot to me that you're still talking to me after all this. It's very comforting.

To: SuperCuteTXNGirl75

From: LoneShepherdinMI73

Subject: RE: Encounter

Date: July 15, 2000

Dear Kelly,

I know it's been a while since we've talked. I don't think you replied to my last message, but I need to tell someone about what happened.

Following the evening I saw the creature stand on its hind legs, I decided to sell my flock before more of them could be brutally slaughtered. It took a week, but I finally found someone interested in buying them. I didn't see the creature during that week, but I knew it wasn't gone. I don't know how I knew that, but I did. This whole situation wasn't about food or territory—there was something else to this.

So, the buyer came over and inspected the sheep. We discussed a few numbers and he asked why I was selling off the flock. I just told him I wasn't interested in sheep anymore, and that I was willing to sell him the herding dogs as well. He seemed interested, but he said he had to look over his books first. I wanted to move all the sheep out at once, which isn't cheap, so he had to check a few things first to make sure he *could* do it. He left just around dusk.

As I was cleaning up from the day, the evening began to warm up, and since the ground was damp, a thick fog rolled in and as it neared its thickest, a chill went down my spine. I turned and sure enough, on the far end of the property, making the flock stampede my way, was a pair of glowing yellow eyes. They were from a high point and moved closer slowly—it must have already been on two legs.

I ran for my house and bolted the door. I hadn't run so much because I was terrified, but because I had a plan this time. During the past week, I had melted down some authentic silverware, and because silver doesn't get along real well with rifling, I merely dunked the tips of my ammo in it. Then, through an old friend down at the gun range, I was able to acquire a new binary substance that explodes when shot at high velocity and an old WWII piece that the ATF wouldn't want me to have. I posted up inside my house and turned off all the lights. I'm sure this thing can see in the dark, but there's no sense helping it.

I stuck my M1 out the back kitchen window, and prepared to aim at one of the spots where I had the substance hidden, but I had to stop as I couldn't see through the fog. Add to that, I didn't see the creature. I couldn't see its eyes anywhere. I would've run from room to room looking, but I wanted to force the thing to approach me from one direction. Based on its behavior from the previous week, I had the sneaking suspicion that it wanted me to watch it as it killed my sheep. But now, I couldn't see the creature anywhere.

I held onto my gun more tightly, just in case it was sneaking up on me and was going to try to take it when I heard a tapping on one of my windows down at the other side of the house. There were three very clear taps. They made the same sound from the night I had heard it in bed.

After a pause, three more taps came, but this time from a closer window. There was another pause, and then another three taps on an even closer window. They all came from the other side of the house, which wasn't far away as the house isn't that wide. I looked over my shoulder, past my dogs cowering behind me, and watched my living room windows intently. *Tap, tap, tap.* That was from the next room. *Tap, tap, tap.* That was on the living room's furthest window. I followed the pace of the pauses with my eyes, but I still jumped when I heard the three taps on the window directly across from me, and again from a height well above my head.

I followed the pause again to my next window, this one on the side of the house to my right, but there weren't any more taps. I slowly pulled my gun from the window and turned around to face my living room. I aimed down the sights and waited.

Suddenly, I detected shuffling from around my feet. I looked and saw my dogs back into the kitchen cabinets directly across from me, their whines reaching a fevered pitch. Something then pulled me back into the kitchen sink. I shot and dropped my gun out of surprise. I turned to look and saw this great, black, hairy arm reaching through my window, holding me by my shirt, and I thought I was going to die of shock!

The creature yanked again and I was pulled up and back onto the sink. If it tried pulling me back through the window, I was going to be mangled through the small opening for sure. I grabbed a pistol I had also prepared, put the muzzle right on the creature's arm and pulled the trigger!

The creature's arm jumped, which jerked me around as a deafening roar came from outside. The creature let go and I fell off the sink. I turned around just in time to see two yellow eyes burning with fury as the creature bellowed through the window. It stuck its arm through the window again, and before I could jump back, it snatched me by the shirt and pulled me forward with all of its might. My face hit the window, and I came eye-to-eye with the beast.

It tugged again, smashing my head against the glass, breaking it. I raised my gun and fired, shattering the window. The creature let go again, and I fell to the floor. I felt like I was winning, but it was hard to tell, especially since without the window, the creature could now stick its entire head into my kitchen. My blood ran cold as the shadow of its head with those two yellow eyes loomed over me. My dogs soiled themselves and as I tried to sink into the floor, something dug into my back. I remembered the M1 and lifted it. The creature tried to retreat, but I got off a few shots before it disappeared out of the window.

I rose and fired blindly out the window as the creature started to run off, but a stray round managed to find one of the exploding canisters and blew up. The creature howled, and following the explosion, I heard a loud thump overhead as the creature jumped onto my roof. Acting on the plan I had already conceived and not thinking about what I was doing, I grabbed the gun my friend lent me—a Sturmgewehr 44—and I fired thirty fully automatic rounds into the roof where I thought the creature was.

I was about to reload when I heard the sound of creaking wood. My eyes went wide as I realized what was about to happen. My roof caved in and 1000 lbs of monster fell through. It landed on my kitchen table, splintering it, and it roared. It reached out with both hands and snatched Apollo and Ziggy. What came next was a sound I never want to hear again as flesh tore and bones broke mixing with yelps that were suddenly cut short. The anger threatened to overwhelm me, but the fear already had. I grabbed Lady by the collar and with her whining, I dragged her outside as fast as I could and I made a half-assed attempt to blockade the door with a feed bag. Looking back, it was entirely stupid because the creature had already proved it could jump onto my roof.

Anyway, I grabbed Lady by the collar again and dragged her to the front of my house as quickly as I could. Without any other option, I headed for my truck and planned on never returning. But then something struck me, and I don't mean physically, but rather…telepathically? I don't know how to explain it exactly, but something told me to wait and turn around. I did, and I faced my living room window. Somehow the shade had disappeared and I saw the creature standing in my living room in its full glory. It locked eyes with me and chills shot throughout my body, but nothing could have prepared me for what happened next. Its mouth dropped open and it almost seemed to grin, and I had the creeping feeling that the more terrified I became, the more it enjoyed my fear in some perverse way.

I wanted nothing more than to turn away from the creature, to leave then and there and never look back! But I couldn't…it wasn't in my power to break eye contact. But then—fortunately and *un*fortunately—I was shaken out of the stupor by a howl. It was the same kind of howl I had heard from this creature, but it was slightly different. And before I laid eyes on it—or rather, *them*—I already knew that there were more of these things. And sure enough, stalking out of the woodline fifty yards past the road, about a dozen pairs of glowing yellow eyes appeared.

I didn't look back at the creature as I already knew it was enjoying my palpable fear, and I just rushed to my truck. I pushed Lady in, and doing my best to ignore the encircling monsters, I left the farm behind.

I haven't been back to the house since, and according to my neighbors, they said it looks like a pack of wolves has ravaged the area. All the sheep are dead, the house is wrecked beyond repair, and gnawed dog bones litter my kitchen. They managed to get what I really wanted, which were my firearms, whatever money I had left, and a few important documents, especially those needed to sell the property.

I don't know what the creatures wanted with that land, but they can have it. At least I now know why the last owner wanted to get rid of it so badly, but that doesn't explain why they were absent for so long or why they suddenly disappeared again.

Whatever. I don't want to think about it anymore. Unfortunately, I feel like I've been marked. Any time I go outside, I get that eerie being-watched feeling. And most dogs look at me and Lady funny. I really wish this hadn't happened to me.

I'm sure you don't believe me, but I hope you do. And I really hope to hear from you again. I guess we'll have to wait and see. But...I don't think I'll ever go back into the woods.

Sincerely,

Rawlin Jones

          Are you sure you want to delete this message?

                        Yes   No

The Serpent

Prologue

The young man tried to recline in his seat. He didn't understand how some people slept on a plane. Despite the luxury of being the only one in his row and right next to the window, he could not get comfortable. And the storm outside wasn't helping. Rain pelted the window, dark clouds filled the skyline, and lightning would brighten the darkened cabin. It seemed as if the skies were conspiring against him.

"Here's your pillow, Dr. Dorian," said a stewardess from his left.

"Thank you. Um, do you know when we'll be landing?"

"Despite the rain, the captain says we'll be arriving in Ontonagon right on time. Don't worry." She smiled before walking away.

Dorian wasn't worried about arriving on time—he was worried about arriving at all. Not just because of the storm, but because he still couldn't believe he had agreed to do this.

Ontonagon. It was a small village of barely 1,500 in Michigan's Upper Peninsula on the southwestern edge of Lake Superior. It was supposed to be a picturesque hamlet in the middle of the Michigan wilderness. It was barely more than a tourist trap, though from what he had gleaned online, its popularity had diminished greatly over the past six years. He didn't care to find out why, but if it had anything to do with why he was going there, perhaps this trip wouldn't be a bust after all.

Despite how much Dorian despised the idea of the expedition he had agreed to, his life since graduation hadn't been ideal. Sure, there had been some highlights, such as the paleontological expedition in South America, but it was because of that dig that he had been sought out for this one. It could've been worse, but the life of a marine zoologist could've been better. Now, he was wrapped up in some sort of Loch Ness Monster hunt, lest he rest on his laurels and lose his nomination for the Deep Sea Research Project.

Dorian leaned his head back and closed his eyes. His mind drifted to Cordelia. He could picture her clearly: her loving smile, her big brown eyes, and her long, curly, reddish-brown hair. He clutched the locket that hung from his neck that contained her ashes. She had died less than a month ago.

Cordelia had been the reason Dorian went for his Ph.D., and she was the reason he continued now. That's not to say that sharks and whales weren't interesting, but it had been she who showed him the great ethereal beauty of the deep. But ever since her death, the ocean, seas, and lakes of the world held substantially less wonder for him. Now, he was compelled to explore and explain their mysteries simply to honor her memory, and he hated himself for it. She deserved a better living legacy than him.

Dorian found himself standing at the edge of a vast lake. He had never been here before, but for some reason, it seemed familiar.

All too surprisingly for Dorian, he was at eye level with the surface of the water. He could see it roll up and down with small waves here and there. For him, this was the most frightening angle he could be at with any body of water. It appeared completely blue and hid whatever lay beneath its surface. He felt a chill as he considered the possibilities and tried to draw back, but he couldn't. Something compelled him to move his face through the bulwark and see what was beneath the waves.

Dorian took the plunge, but instead of seeing beneath the waves, he now found himself floating in the sky above the same body of water at night. He had no explanation for it, and as he looked around, he could see the true expanse of the lake. It reached up to and beyond the horizon in every direction. Something caught Dorian's eye and as he looked down, he was stunned to see a large, serpentine shadow moving beneath the surface. Periodic lightning strikes helped to illuminate the size of the shadow better. Dorian couldn't put an estimate on its length or girth since he didn't know how high he was, but the shadow stretched almost right up to the horizon. How could anything be *that* big? He should have felt safe, so high in the sky, but he didn't—he felt exposed, because he knew that whatever that thing was could pluck him out from the sky.

That's when the sky turned orange and Dorian heard the roar of flames. He turned and behind him was a burning forest. He could feel the intensity of the fire on the surface of his skin despite being several yards away. He shielded his face and turned back toward the lake, but he didn't see the lake anymore. Instead, it was a fetid bog. A massive, sickly, stinking swamp. The water was thick and grey with what appeared to be reeds or logs sticking out of it, but Dorian didn't look at them too closely as something more interesting caught his eye. Occasionally, he would catch a brief glance of something big and black, roiling through the muck. It appeared to be a snake's coil, but it was large—larger than any snake—and possibly any whale—on Earth. Each time Dorian saw one of its coils, he became chilled and uneasy as if he had just walked in on two people having sex. This was something he wasn't supposed to be seeing. An eldritch truth of the world was being revealed to him, and the insight of it was enough to drive him mad.

That's when the whole world went red. Dorian looked around and he saw thousands upon thousands of red lights lining the sky, all directed at him. Dorian examined them and realized that they weren't lights, but rather eyes because every so often, they would twitch, and Dorian could feel their gaze pierce through him. That's when the spaces in between turned black and started opening to reveal hundreds upon hundreds of slavering, drooling mouths lined with rows upon rows of razor sharp teeth.

Dorian felt like he was going to scream. He knew he had to run, but he didn't know where he could run to. He tried to angle his body downward and head for the swamp, but that's when he saw and heard something else. The swamp had changed into a writhing mass of dull grey and bluish colors. He couldn't understand what he was looking at until he realized the sound he was hearing was the drone of moaning. He was looking at a crowd of people, but they weren't normal people. They were all disfigured in horrible ways. Some looked drowned, while others were missing their skin, and a group of six nearest to him all had stretched necks with heads that drooped to one side. Dorian didn't want to speculate why they all looked like that, but he had a nagging feeling as to why in the back of his head. It wasn't until he saw a familiar face amongst the crowd that he realized the truth.

"Cordelia!" he gasped.

Cordelia saw him and gasped back. She mouthed some words to him, but he couldn't see what she was trying to say.

And then his sight went dark again followed by a solitary red light. Dorian saw the moon as it glowed red. It was illuminating the lake beneath him and the serpentine shadow reappeared, but Dorian felt as if it had never truly left. It had always been there—it was in the swamp, it was in the sky with the eyes and mouths, and it was there amongst the dead, but why was it here now?

The shadow stopped and seemed to angle upward toward him. Dorian shielded himself with his arms, but he felt compelled to look. Something was urging him—*forcing* him—to look. Dorian could no longer take the pressure on his mind and he looked back up at the moon, but it appeared differently from before. It was still red, but it wasn't shaped like the moon. It was more like one of the thousands of eyes and seemed to be set into the darkness of the sky.

Dorian was bathed in the red glow, and he felt the attention of the whole world. Or, that's what he thought. It wasn't the whole world, but rather a solitary being whose mental presence was so large that it felt like the whole world. Dorian looked up and saw the source of the red light twitch, and he knew he had the serpent's attention and that it was the very last thing he could ever want.

Dorian jumped, screaming.

"Are you all right, Dr. Dorian?!" said the stewardess alarmed. Several other passengers on the plane were also agitated.

Dorian looked around wide-eyed. "Wha—where—?!"

"Are you all right?" the stewardess asked again.

Dorian took a few raspy breaths, and managed to calm down. "Yes..." he said at last. "I'm fine. Just a nightmare...I think."

The stewardess smiled. "There, there. Would you like something to help you relax?"

"No," said Dorian, wiping the sweat from his face. "I'm fine."

Dorian reclined back, ashamed and embarrassed, but still troubled by what he had just seen. Was that Hell? Was Cordelia in Hell?! And that thing that looked like the moon—was that an eye? Had Dorian seen some sort of giant snake at the bottom of that lake? Chills overwhelmed his body and sweat drenched his face. He clutched the locket again, and stared out the window. He refused to sleep until they reached Ontonagon.

Day 1

Dorian hadn't slept well, even after the hassle of getting off the plane, getting his luggage, and checking into the hotel. He was tired, but couldn't sleep. The nightmare he'd had on the plane still plagued him. He'd never had a dream like that before. He did his best to block it out, but that only made him think about it more. The flames, the eyes, the moon, the monster, and the ghosts of the dead. Did it all have something to do with why he was here?

When dawn came, he was relieved. He changed his clothes and headed for a nearby diner where he was supposed to meet the other members of the expedition.

Dorian entered the diner and approached the hostess' podium. "I'm supposed to be meeting with a Mr. Paul Burke."

"Ah! Dr. Dorian!" said a middle-aged man with black hair and a beard and glasses with wide, round rims. "Down here, man!"

Dorian nodded to the hostess and walked down the aisle of tables until he came to a corner booth loaded with five men. Dorian recoiled at first, until he realized they all seemed to be just as uncomfortable with the situation as he was. Burke was the only one smiling.

"Sit down! Sit down, Dorian!" he waved to the end of the booth. "It's a pleasure to finally meet you in person!"

"Thanks," said Dorian, sitting next to a man in a fishing vest.

"Now, that everyone is here," began Burke, "we can get started."

"With breakfast?" said a man with a harsh, deep voice and a slight grizzled appearance despite his young features.

"Um, yes? I suppose? But what I really meant was the meeting…"

Burke didn't get to finish as a waitress appeared.

"Excellent," said the grizzled young man. "I'll have…"

Dorian looked at each of his companions, noting their behaviors and mannerisms as they ordered. The one who had asked about breakfast was blunt, but there was also something about him that was straight-edged. Was he a police officer or former military?

The one sitting next to him was another young man with a slender and scrappy build. His voice was higher, but he was by no means wimpy. There was even an undertone to his voice that hinted at him being smarter than he appeared. But the next one sitting between him and Burke did not seem bright. He was pale with a round face and liked to say "man" a lot. He didn't seem like a pothead, just a guy who listened to too much heavy metal when he was younger.

Finally, the fisherman sitting next to Dorian was soft-spoken and polite. He was also the oldest one there, probably in his sixties.

"And for you, hun?" said the waitress to Dorian.

"Coffee. Black."

"That's it?" asked Burke.

"I'll be drinking a lot of it," Dorian assured.

The waitress rolled her eyes and walked away.

"Now, then, gentlemen," began Burke, beaming, "we all know why we're here. We're here on a search for truth and adventure, the likes of which may alter the course of world and zoological history. But what we don't know is why each one of us is here, other than the fact that I invited you all personally. So, I shall begin the introductions…

"I am Paul Burke, but you already knew that. I was a wildlife photographer for more than twenty years up until a few years ago when I saw my first cryptid."

"A what?" asked the round-faced man.

"It's a scientifically undocumented animal," explained the scrappy one. "Like Bigfoot or the Loch Ness Monster."

"Indeed," said Burke. "Now, not many know what I saw, and from the investigations I've done myself, I've found very little evidence of it, but what I can promise you is that it wasn't like anything you've seen before. But by delving into its mysteries, I became enrapt with the world of unknown animals and thus began my life's greatest passion. Since, I've done investigations on Bigfoot, el Chupacabra, the Lizardman, the Mothman, and the Jersey Devil. My travels have taken me to many remote places, and despite some of the chills and thrills that have taken a number of years off my old ticker, it's been an absolute joy!"

"You ever find anything?" asked the harsh voiced man.

"If I told you, I would have to kill you," finished Burke, still beaming.

The man grunted. "I've heard that before."

"Why don't you introduce yourself, Drake?"

"Okay," Drake said with a shrug. "My name is Mark Drake, and Burke here hired me to operate the sonar and be a part of the diving team."

"Have you had much experience using sonar?" asked Dorian suddenly.

"I've done several tours with the Navy."

"Oh? That should be sufficient."

"For what?"

"For operating the sonar."

Drake pouted at Dorian as a few of the others also gave him strange looks.

"Hicks…" prodded Burke.

"I'm Michael Hicks," said the scrappy man. "I'm a Michigan native who moved to the Upper Peninsula when I was ten. I'm the group's historian. I've done most of the legend hunting for this adventure."

"I'll go next, man," said the round-faced man next to Hicks. "I'm Billy Hudson. I'll be operating the underwater camera and hydrophone."

Dorian raised his eyebrows. "A hydrophone? Burke, I can understand the camera, but a hydrophone? What for?"

"Some theories suggest that many lake serpents are mammals, and so they may communicate via echolocation. There are actually recordings of echolocation taken from Lake Champlain in New York and even Loch Ness, which gave rise to these theories. And no recorded animal in those waters is supposed to be able to echolocate."

Dorian furrowed his brow. He didn't believe it. Even if he had heard the recordings himself, he still wouldn't believe it. He turned back to Hudson. "How much experience do you have using all that equipment?"

"Plenty, man. I've worked for NOAA."

"The National Oceanic and Atmospheric Administration? Damn. This crew is more technical and specialized than I thought."

"Except for me," said the elderly man next to him. "I'm Lance Fox. I'm just a local fisherman."

"Lance is being modest," explained Burke. "He knows these waters like the back of his hand!"

Lance shrugged. "I guess you could say that. I've been fishing all over the Great Lakes, especially Lake Superior. I know every fish in there."

"Anything in these waters come close to what we're looking for?" asked Dorian.

Lance shook his head. "Nope. The only one amongst us that's had a sighting is Michael."

Everyone turned to Hicks.

"That's true," said Burke, "but before we go there, we have one more personality to introduce." He looked at Dorian.

"Um, well, I'm Dr. James Dorian."

"What are you a doctor of?" asked Drake. "I can't imagine us needing a surgeon on this mission."

"My Ph.D. is in marine zoology from the University of Miami."

Hicks grunted. "A marine zoologist could be really helpful on his adventure."

"I fail to see how…"

"Because you'll be able to tell us what sort of animal we're dealing with."

"If it's what I suspect, any child in the world can tell you what an eel looks like."

"There are no eels in Lake Superior," added Lance. "The sturgeon do get mighty big, though."

"So, you're a skeptic, Dr. Dorian?" said Hicks.

"Yes."

"Then why are you here?"

"Ah!" said Burke. "Dr. Dorian is most distinguished amongst his colleagues. He is slated to be one of only a handful of people who will be working at the South Pacific Research Facility."

The others looked at him expectedly.

Dorian sighed. "I've been invited to take part in the Deep Sea Research Project."

"The one where they're building research facilities on the ocean floor?" asked Lance.

"Correct," said Dorian. "The South Pacific facility will be off the coast of Chile."

"But they're not supposed to be finished until 2065."

Dorian shrugged. "That's only five years away."

"How'd you get that distinction?" asked Drake.

"Couple of years ago I was part of a paleontological research team in Chile that was looking for extinct marine reptiles. During a dig, we came across a full fossilized skeleton of an unknown sea reptile."

"Wait a second," said Hudson. "I think I heard about this in the news. There was something strange about the skeleton, wasn't there? Like, someone said it looked like the 'Biblical Leviathan'?"

"Yes…" sighed Dorian. "One of the grad students said that. It was an unusual find because it didn't look like anything we've seen before. Dr. Cope said he thought it could be an early ancestor of the Tylosaurus. But the reason it shook the paleontology community was because of its dragon-like skull. It wasn't long and narrow like a regular marine reptile's head. It was shorter and almost ended in an overbite like a crocodile's. And it had several horns sticking out the back of its head. Strangely, though, I've heard it's gone missing…"

"I thought dragons *were* reptiles," said Drake.

"Depends on who you ask," replied Burke. "Some people consider them to be a type of 'serpent', which can be a vague term for anything long and snake-like."

"And so finding this dragon-like marine reptile is how you secured your position at the deep sea research facility?" asked Hicks.

"That and I was the only one from the team that didn't have any prior commitments five years from now. Additionally, the investors were interested in seeing if there's anything alive today in that same area that has gone undiscovered. Thinking me an expert, they supported my nomination."

"But that's not all!" said Burke. "You were also quoted in an interesting article in an issue of *Marine Life* magazine."

"Yeah…" said Dorian, sighing again. "Back in Miami we were testing claims that dolphins are psychic. We left children that couldn't swim in a tank of water. They had life jackets and we were nearby, so they weren't in any real danger, but they were still in distress. It was our hope that the dolphins would save the children by pushing them to the edge of the tank where we could grab them.

"We developed other tests, but I can't really tell you anything about them as I wasn't in charge of the experiments. Hell, I barely understood the pseudoscience mumbo-jumbo that the head researcher was throwing around. But the other tests included testing the psychic prowess of other marine animals including whales, certain kinds of fish, and even sharks. In some of the tests, both the whales' and sharks' results were better than random. So, I said that *in theory* it's possible that sharks are psychic. *Marine Life* grabbed onto that quote and used it to headline the article. So—"

"So, you're no stranger to marine paranormal phenomenon?" said Hicks.

"Indeed!" said Burke. "And that's why I asked him to join us."

"Look," said Dorian, "it was just a theory, and I barely believe that dolphins are psychic. Hell, I don't believe in human psychics. And I don't believe in sea monsters." The shadow of the serpent and the red moon flashed through his mind, giving him chills.

"But, you must have some interest in the subject," concluded Hicks. "Look where you are. And by your own free will."

Burke got excited.

Dorian's eyes narrowed. "It's for my career."

Hudson and Drake both furrowed their brows at Dorian.

"Sounds like this sort of expedition could hurt your career," said Drake. "The scientific community scoffs at this sort of thing."

"True, but if I spin it as I'm looking for more lost relatives of the extinct animal found in Chile, the investors will eat it up."

"That's ironic," laughed Hicks. "Building your career on an animal you don't believe exists."

Dorian shrugged. "Stranger things have happened."

With introductions out of the way, Burke decided to start in earnest. "Now, then, gentlemen, let's get down to some real business. You all know that we are here to hunt down the elusive cryptid known as the Superior Serpent!"

Dorian had a flashback to the night before and started sweating.

"It is a creature surrounded in mystery and speculation. Hicks! Why don't you tell us what we should know?"

"The creature we're hunting has its origins in Native American myth. The Ojibwe called it the 'mishiginebig', which translates to 'great serpent', and was said to have horns on its head and eat humans."

Dorian had another flashback and was enveloped in chills.

"It was a natural enemy of the Thunderbirds. There are numerous other legends, but they all boil down to the Serpent either being dangerous or a trickster. And if the eyewitness reports are accurate, that sounds about right."

"How many reports are there?" asked Hudson.

"More than their fair share," answered Burke. "Speaking of, I have a number of contacts here," he said, pulling a few papers from his briefcase. "All of them are eyewitnesses from the surrounding area. Since we don't have the boat today, it was my hope we could partner up and investigate a number of these," he said, passing around the contacts. "Lance, you and I will take the eastern side of town. Drake and Hudson, you will take the west side of town. And Dorian and Hicks, take the beach, dock, and other locales outside of town."

"The first day of our investigation is interviewing locals?" said Dorian.

"Correct. Any good paranormal investigation follows the testimony of those who have seen the 'creature'. Speaking of, Hicks, why don't you tell us about your sighting?"

Hicks swallowed. "Well, a few months back, I was part of an archaeological dig in the ruins of the Porcupine Mountains National Park."

"Ruins?" interjected Dorian.

"Yeah," said Lance. "A few years ago, a man named Timothy Lynch set the whole park on fire."

"Why?" said Drake.

"No one really knows," explained Hicks. "The only thing we really know is that he was racist against Native Americans. At some time either before or during the blaze, he lynched six descendents of the Ojibwe tribe."

"What happened to him?" asked Dorian.

"No one knows for sure, but there were human remains found not too far from the 'killing grounds' that had been charred to a crisp. It's believed that was Lynch."

"Freaky. But, if the national park was torched, what were you doing the dig for?"

"Some kids had managed to break into the park and found some lost artifacts. Their parents found them playing with them and turned them over to the Historical Society. When we heard the story, we obtained the permits necessary to dig at the location where the children had found the artifacts.

"We had been at it for a few weeks when one day we found an object that didn't seem like a regular artifact. We did scans of the ground and found it was a box about a foot long, wide, and deep. There was something inside it, but we couldn't ascertain what. As we began to unearth it, something broke the surface of the lake. We turned and saw this great, black serpent only about twenty yards offshore. It was the biggest thing I've ever seen in the lake. Twenty—maybe thirty feet long. More than two feet in diameter, with a row of pointed spines down its back. It was incredible!"

Dorian was chilled again.

"But, the thing about it that really struck us wasn't how big it was, but rather how it made us feel. When we saw it, each of us felt incredibly small and completely terrified. We had the feeling we were seeing something so ancient that modern man was not supposed to know that it existed."

Dorian's skin burst into cold sweats.

"Dread overcame each of us, and before we knew what we were doing, all of us had turned and run for the Jeeps. We got out of there as fast as we could and didn't look back."

There was a pause as Hicks finished his story. Everyone seemed to be in a reflective state, even Dorian until his rational mind rushed to his rescue.

"How many of you were on that dig?" he suddenly asked.

"Um, seven, I think."

"And you're the only one to come forward?"

"The others were too terrified to make formal statements. And, I was the only one to research the creature and that's how I found out about the mishiginebig. About a day or two later, I tripped over Burke's website and sent him a message. He contacted me a few days later and wanted to launch an expedition immediately."

"Immediately?" repeated Dorian, looking at Burke.

"I wanted to strike while the iron was hot!" he replied.

"I see..." Dorian turned back to Hicks. "What of the dig site and the box you mentioned?"

"We left everything there after the sighting. I did later return with a sheriff's escort to collect our equipment and whatever artifacts we had uncovered, but I didn't go back to the box, so it's still there as far as I know."

"Anyone else besides Burke and the other diggers know about what you saw?"

Hicks swallowed again. "Sort of... I told the city council and the sheriff's office that we were attacked by an unknown animal. Some of them suggested Bigfoot or something called 'the Dogman', but I remained vague about what we saw. I really didn't want to go back, but someone had to in order to grab our equipment."

"Why didn't you want to go back? I mean, correct me if I'm wrong, but a lake serpent is in the lake, and doesn't have legs. So, what were you scared of?"

"Like I said, we all got an intense feeling of dread. We all felt mortally in danger. One of the others says she felt like she was standing on the precipice of Hell. And when I went back, both the sheriff and I felt really uncomfortable being there. The site was eerily quiet, and it was cold even though the day wasn't. It was also sad, like the feeling you get when you spend too much time in a graveyard. Something was not right."

Dorian stared at Hicks as parts of his brains waged war against each other. His rational brain wanted to pose theory after theory and poke hole after hole, but with the memory of the nightmare still fresh in his mind, his rational mind couldn't reach his mouth, especially after the mention of "standing on the precipice of Hell". That wording was too accurate to Dorian's nightmare. He forced his mouth open to speak, but he was interrupted by the arrival of the waitress and their food.

***

After breakfast, they split up as Burke had directed with Dorian and Hicks heading away from the town.

"I'm looking forward to this," said Hicks as he looked over the contact names. "It will be affirming to know other people have seen what I have. Maybe you'll see it yourself on this expedition."

"Not likely," said Dorian, although, some part of him really hoped he wouldn't. The nightmare still loomed large in his mind.

They crossed the bridge over the Ontonagon River and headed to the outskirts of town. Of the first three people they tried, one wasn't home and the other two claimed not to know anything about the creature or even reporting the sighting. Most of their eyewitnesses could only vaguely describe the creature as a long shadow in the water. Some didn't even really claim to see it so much as they saw its wake. One eyewitness had footage, but there wasn't anything in the frame for scale, despite the fellow claiming the creature was over forty feet long. But one thing that all the eyewitnesses did report was a feeling of dread or terror as if coming to grips with their own untimely demise. That one detail stuck out the most among others, but Dorian still couldn't take the eyewitnesses seriously as most of them could've been dubbed "white trash" or "rubes".

"Yeah, I seen it," said the eyewitness, they were interviewing. "It was as long as a school bus and twice my heft!"

Dorian found that hard to believe. This particular eyewitness must've been at least 350 pounds. He was so wide in the waist that he had to lean back to balance out the weight of his belly. He also wheezed as he breathed, and kept moving his arms and hands around. Not so much to gesticulate as he spoke, but because he couldn't find the most comfortable position to put them in. The man looked as if he wasn't used to standing. Dorian and Hicks interviewed him on his porch.

"Are there any distinguishing details you can give us?" asked Hicks.

"Distinguishing? Oh, you mean was there anything special about the way it looked. Well, as far as I can tell you, it was just big and black. And it swum like a snake, back and forth," said the man, moving his hand from side-to-side.

"Did you see its head?"

"Naw, was too afraid to look to be honest."

"Afraid?"

"Yeah… That's the thing that gets me still, not so much that it was a big bastard the likes of which I ain't never seen in the Superior, but more of the fear I felt when I saw it. My whole body went cold and I was paralyzed. All I could do was watch as this thing passed our boat. There was something real creepy about the whole experience, like taking a walk through a graveyard at night. Something about it just don't feel right.

"Anyway, just as the tail end of him was coming up, he submerged into the water and disappeared. Thankfully, it had been raining a few days since, so the water wasn't real clear. He disappeared only a few feet down, and I was glad to see him go."

"Interesting," said Hicks. "Dorian, do you have anything to add?"

Dorian shook his head. There were follow-up questions he wanted to ask, but the smell of the man and the unkempt condition of his yard and home were starting to irritate him.

"Very well, then. Thank you, Mr. Garterbough."

Once Dorian and Hicks were a few yards away, Dorian said, "Good grief! That man was ugly! And fat! And smelly!"

"Yes, he was unpleasant. But, man, what's with you? You're not contributing to this investigation at all."

"What's there to contribute so far? 'Sir, what did you see? Something long and dark. What else? It scared the shit out of me. Want to see the stains?' Seriously, that's all we have on this creature so far. Do you really believe these people?"

"I believe they saw something."

"Do you believe they saw the Superior Serpent?"

"Well…there's nothing else in those waters that matches these descriptions, as vague as they are. And that last one, I know what he means by the fear."

"Having your preconceived notions about the world shattered can do that to you," said Dorian. "As can seeing a gigantic predator in front of you for the first time. Something primal within you freaks out. I've had the same feeling many times when facing down sharks."

"It wasn't either of those. Like Mr. Garterbough said, there was something unnatural to the fear. Something about it was unwholesome. Like I said, seeing this thing is somehow a violation of the natural world, like coming too close to the veil that separates us from death."

Dorian grunted. He wanted to argue, but the sentiment of coming too close to the dead spoke to him. He couldn't help but think of Cordelia. He grabbed the locket around his neck. No one had asked about it, but he was grateful. He was embarrassed for being so sentimental.

"Anyway," said Hicks, "we only have two eyewitnesses left, and one's across from the other. Here," he said, handing Dorian the case file. "Make yourself useful and go ask them some questions."

Dorian grimaced as he took the file. He crossed the street to a solitary white house. Like the others he had seen, it was suitably rundown with a burned grass front and backyard, a screen that was loose in one corner in the front window, and it had an ever growing stockade of children's discarded yard toys on the side. He glanced at the name in the file as he climbed the front porch. He knocked unceremoniously, and when the door opened, without looking up, said, "Is Mr…Hendrid? Hendrid?! Um, is Mr. Hendrid O. Cold at home?"

When no response came, Dorian looked up, but saw no one other than the dark interior of the house. Something reached up into the bottom of his peripheral and he jumped as he saw a little girl raising her hand on the screen door. She stared at him with big blue eyes.

"Oh. Uh…"

"You want to talk to Uncle Henry?" asked the girl.

"Um…I suppose."

"What you want to talk about?"

"He saw something in the lake and I wanted to ask him a few questions about it."

"Oh!" said the girl. "You want to hear his monster story. The story that Momma says made him crazy."

Dorian started. "I'm sorry."

"He saw something scary in the lake. He said he came face-to-face with a monster. He's still my uncle, but not like he used to be. He's different now.

He says things in a low inside voice, even when there's no one talking to him. Papa says he talks to the wall because no one else will listen."

It wasn't in Dorian's nature to parley with a child, but from how earnest Hicks was about his experience, he was more than a little curious to know what sort of creature could cause a psychotic breakdown. "Tell me…sweetheart," he forced a smile on his face, "what did your uncle see?"

"I'm not supposed to talk about it. Momma doesn't like to hear about it. But, from what I've heard my uncle whisper, he called it a monster and a demon. He also called it a dragon once, but I've never heard of a dragon living in the water."

"A dragon?" repeated Dorian. That sounded like an approximate description of a horned serpent. "Where is Uncle Henry now…darling? May I speak to him?"

"Nuh-uh. He isn't here no more. Momma and Papa took him somewhere. Somewhere they said where he could get all the rest he needed."

Dorian recoiled. An insane asylum. His interest was piqued now.

"Who are you talking to, pumpkin?" said a woman as she came from the back.

"Oh, just a man who's asking about Uncle Henry?"

"Uncle Henry?!" The color drained from the woman's face.

"Indeed," said Dorian. "I would like to speak with him about what he saw in the lake."

The woman bristled like a startled cat before scooping up the girl. "He didn't see anything! Now, go away!" she shouted, slamming the door.

Dorian rolled his eyes and descended the porch. He crossed the street and met up with Hicks as he was leaving his interview.

"Get anything?" asked Hicks.

Dorian explained what happened. Hicks' eyes widened and he stood stock still.

"That's…creepy," he said.

"It is, but I find it difficult to believe that seeing something out of the ordinary would turn someone stark-raving mad."

"But you haven't seen what this guy saw. So, how can you criticize him for losing his mind?"

Dorian stared at Hicks. "You didn't go insane when you saw it."

"I didn't see its face." Hicks sighed. "I can't imagine how horrifying that must've been."

Dorian grunted.

They crossed the bridge back into Ontonagon proper. Dorian looked behind Hicks at the mouth of the river where it emptied into Lake Superior. He saw a series of waves swell up headed for the river mouth. In one of them, something shadowy caught Dorian's eye. As he focused on it, he felt something deep within his being start to give away as he had a flashback to his nightmare. But before he could allow the sighting of the wave reach his logical brain, he ripped his gaze from the lake.

"So, are we going to meet back up with the others?" he said in a strained tone.

***

After briefly meeting back at the diner to divulge what they had found, which wasn't much of anything and all sounded the same, Burke gave them the rest of the day off, but encouraged them to study anything they could about their query. Dorian ignored that and returned to his hotel room. He sat on the bed with his back to the window, which faced the lake. He was still irritated that he had agreed to do this, and the longer he sat, the more he began to teem with frustration. He didn't know why, but he dared not look at the lake. He convinced himself that it was because he hoped the thing didn't exist, and some part of him feared it did.

Dorian tried to preoccupy his mind by reading articles on the Net about the recent discoveries of the world's oceans, whether it was about new creatures, fauna, or geographical features. In the building of the deep sea research facilities, many new things had been discovered that had never been seen before. But these searches for new information led nowhere; nothing new had been discovered recently.

He found meaningless ways to spend the time, often pacing his room. Every time he thought about going out or going down to the beach front, he would become agitated and his hands would shake. He wanted to go outside, but also very much didn't want to leave the safety of his room.

When the hour grew late and the night dark, he was grateful and prepared for bed. He lay down but didn't turn off the lamp or shut his eyes. Every time he blinked or rubbed his eyes, he saw something that upset him: a serpentine shadow, a moon glowing red, a burning forest, a sickly bog, or a crowd of lost souls. Occasionally, he would see the shadow that began to form in the wave he saw earlier. He clutched his covers and his breathing quickened. He grabbed the locket around his neck. "Cordelia!... I need you!"

Dorian was suddenly aware of someone standing at the foot of his bed. He sat up and slowly lifted his gaze. As he did so, there was a faint chant echoing in the room. "Sanity rent by madness pure…"

Dorian slowly traced up the shapely thighs of a woman to her hips and waist.

"A cursed death lends to a cursed afterlife. Life is but a dream and death a reality…"

As Dorian reached her chest, he could see she was dripping wet and her skin looked grey. He also recognized the diving suit she wore.

"By divine begot, by betrayal born, by vengeance unleashed…"

Dorian made it to her chin and slowed his gaze as he went over a pair of lips and cheeks he had kissed dozens of times.

"Fear welcomes all, death accepts all fearful…"

He slowed as much as he could when he reached those deep brown eyes he had stared into a thousand times and he clenched down on a scream.

"Seek not the Serpent…"

The look of recognition he saw on Cordelia's face was more ghastly than seeing the entirety of her spectral form. She gasped, and Dorian's mind had had enough.

Dorian's eyes snapped open and his scream was blood-curdling. He panted to the point of hyperventilating, and when he could no longer breathe, he knew he had to calm down. He took several slow, deep breaths and tried to erase the dream from his mind. As he focused, he was able to shut out the image and the creepy chanting, and he was finally able to look up since waking up. The first vestiges of morning were beginning to work their way through his closed blinds. It took him a minute to understand why—he hadn't felt like he had slept the whole night.

He sat up with some stiffness. He had fallen asleep on his back, and his hands were sore as he had been clutching onto the sheets in one hand and the locket with the other for the whole night. Dorian shook his head and wiped the sweat from his face. He shivered as well, revealing his skin covered in goose bumps.

"What was that?!"

Day 2

Dorian met the others down at the docks that morning. A brief sense of anxiety agitated him, but he ignored it as he approached the end of the pier.

"Good morning, Dr. Dorian!" said Burke. "So glad you joined us."

"You say that like I wasn't going to."

"I didn't think you were going to," said Hicks.

"On the contrary, man," said Burke, "I had no doubt you would show up, but I'm glad to see you just the same."

Dorian grunted. "So," he began, looking over the tops of the others, "what're we doing today? Staring at the lake?" He hesitated a little to look around them.

Burke laughed. "Why, no, man. We're waiting for Robert Quint. He's going to be our skipper for this venture. We're waiting for him to come in. He should be along any minute now." Burke turned. "Ah! There he is now! Quint!" he shouted, waving his hand in the air.

Dorian turned and saw a boat about fifty yards away close in. Atop it he saw a middle-aged man in a denim shirt and white ball cap with a thick mustache and mutton chops. The boat in question was a well-worn fishing boat called the Ripley. Despite its appearance, the hull and deck all seemed to be structurally intact. The main deck was a little larger than necessary and the flying bridge had been redone and updated at some point. Its clean, plexiglass renovations didn't match its old-fashioned wooden frame.

The man atop the bridge spun the boat around and backed it along the pier. He shut off his engines before the boat had come to a stop and descended down to the deck. He threw a rope to Hicks, but as Drake and Hudson made a move to board with their equipment, the gnarled captain stood in their way.

"Now, just a second there, boys. I don't let anyone onto my vessel until they agree to my rules."

"Oh, come, come," said Burke. "Is there really any need for this act, Bobby?"

"Call me 'Bobby' again, Burk-y, and I'll keelhaul ya. I only respond to two names aboard my ship: Captain or Quint. Call me anything else, and you'll be swimming home. Understand?

"Now, then, I have two rules for all those aboard my craft. Firstly, it's my ship and I'm the captain. As a result, you'll do everything I tell you. And secondly, you are not allowed to question any of my orders. This may be Burke's charter, but it's my vessel. And so I want you all to think good and hard about what that means. Which one do you think will carry you home safely: Burke's damned passion for creatures that don't exist, or my completely real boat? Well, go on, you tell me."

Each man took it in turn to admit that the Ripley would get them home safe and sound, and not Burke's aspirations.

"Good, with all that agreed upon and understood, welcome aboard."

Quint climbed back up to the flying bridge as Drake and Hudson got busy loading their gear onto the boat. Lance and Hicks helped to secure it all down, while Burke went over the route with Quint. Dorian went to step aboard, but paused. His nightmare from the plane and the one with Cordelia were fresh in his mind. Did he really want to test this? He looked out onto the lake and was overwhelmed by its size. He imagined a frightening shadow and took a step back.

"Dorian!" said Burke from the flying bridge. "What's the matter, man? You look as if you've seen a ghost."

"I do?" The charge disarmed Dorian. He changed the subject. "It's just that, I've been thinking…" he started, trying to keep his voice calm. "If we're looking for something as big as thirty to forty feet, is using an old fishing boat really the best way to go about this? I mean, shouldn't we get a bigger boat? Like that one?" Dorian pointed to a ship farther out in the lake. The rest of the team looked at it.

"Dorian, you mad man," said Hicks. "That's a freighter!"

"It is, isn't it," said Dorian nervously. "Even still, wouldn't a bigger boat work better for our purposes?"

"What?" said Quint. "What's all this, Burke? Thinking of getting yourselves a new captain and boat? That's fine by me, but you're still going to have to pay me for the days I'm not out in the Atlantic."

"No, no," cooed Burke. "We're not doing that. Listen to me, Dorian, I understand your apprehension, but this is all I could afford. Besides, a smaller boat makes for a smaller target in case of aggression."

That didn't make sense to Dorian. He was pretty sure a kayak was a poor choice when looking for Great Whites.

"Think of it this way, man," called Quint, "do you really think we'll find anything? Of course, we won't!"

Burke shot him a dirty look.

Dorian stood there, conflicted. Logically, he agreed with Quint—they wouldn't find anything. But then he remembered his nightmares—there did seem to be something about this, and something never came from nothing. What *were* people seeing out on the water? The desire to answer that question made him lift his foot again, but he still hesitated.

"Oh, enough of this!" said Hicks as he grabbed Dorian and pulled him aboard.

"Hey!"

"There we go!" said Hicks. "We're all set, Quint!"

"Roger!" he said, firing up the engines.

"Why'd you pull me aboard, asshole?!"

"Because you were taking forever. You were going to get on board eventually. I just sped things up."

Dorian wanted to curse him out. He thought about contesting his claim. He thought about jumping over the side and swimming back to the beach just to be difficult, but he was too curious about out what was actually going on. He still decided to err on the side of caution and plant himself on the gunwale near the stern so he could keep an eye on everything as it approached.

They left the dockyard behind and turned west. They went past the neighborhood Hicks and Dorian investigated the day previous and continued out into open water.

"So, where are we going?" asked Dorian when Burke had climbed down to the deck.

"Presque Isle River."

"Uh, I don't think this vessel should go up a river…"

"We're not going up it, man. We're investigating the mouth of it."

"Why?"

"Because that's where I had my sighting," explained Hicks.

"Correct, and Hicks' sighting is the most detailed out of all the ones we have."

Dorian gave Hicks a dubious look, especially given what they had learned the day before. "Are you sure?" asked Dorian.

"Well, perhaps it isn't *the* most detailed, but it is the only one that gives a definite hint about the location of the Superior Serpent."

"Um, Burke? Isn't the *entire* lake a hint about the location of this damn thing?"

"My good fellow, do you have any idea how big Lake Superior is? It is the world's largest freshwater lake by surface area, and the third largest by volume. It covers an area of 31,700 square miles. How would you propose we go about searching for it without some coordinate to follow?"

Dorian shrugged. "I don't know. How do people looking for the Loch Ness Monster go about it?"

Burke shrugged. "The way we intend to go about it: we go to the last known location and drop the hydrophone, sonar, and underwater camera. From there, we'll head north."

"I see."

As they continued west, Dorian could see a large land formation back on shore. It first appeared to be a hill before it swelled into a small mountain range covered by black and ashy masses.

"Is that what I think it is?" asked Dorian.

"That's Porcupine Mountains Wilderness State Park, or it was," said Hicks.

Dorian's mouth dropped. "The cost of the damage must be immense. Not just the dollar amount, but also for the wildlife in the area."

"It was. Thousands of animals perished in the blaze, and those that made it out haven't returned. And there were other people caught in the blaze, too. Tourists, hikers, campers. The death toll was greater than a hundred."

"Have there been any attempts at reforestation?"

"Tried and failed."

"Failed?"

"Nothing seems to want to grow there," explained Hicks. "There aren't even any animals there. It's like the land is cursed. But, considering what happened here, and what I've seen, maybe that's not too far off."

Dorian walked to the edge of the deck and evaluated the devastation of the ruined forest. An entire ecosystem was gone. He could only fathom the ecological side effects.

"And there's the Presque Isle River," said Hicks, pointing. "Which means that's the excavation site."

Dorian looked to where Hicks was pointing. The spot didn't seem special, nor did it even stand out. He could see the hole they dug, but other than that, it all looked the same—black and ashy. Just then, an image flashed through his head. It was of a roaring fire and an orange sky. It was the same image he had had in his nightmare. Except this time, he noticed something new—he saw six bodies hanging from trees in the same spot where Hicks and his team were digging. He smelled burning flesh as a whisper said, "The eyes of the dead conspire against the living…"

The vision was gone as quickly as it came. Dorian plugged his nose at the acrid smell, but as the others looked at him, he realized he was making a scene. He let go of his nose and sniffed.

"Sorry," he said to the others. "Sometimes the smell of fish really gets to me."

"Fish don't smell when they're fresh," noted Lance.

"Something stinks out here. Must be the water." That part wasn't a lie.

"Quint!" called Burke. "We've reached the site. Swing around to the north and slow the boat."

"Roger!"

"Drake and Hudson; drop the hydrophone, sonar, and camera overboard. It's time to begin our search in earnest!"

Drake and Hudson jumped to life and dropped their gear behind the Ripley. They then ran the cords to the cabin where they plugged them into their computers, Hudson donning a pair of headphones.

"Well, boys? Do we have audio and visual?"

"Yep," replied Hudson.

"Aye," said Drake.

"Excellent," said Burke greedily, looking over Drake's shoulder. "Quint! Start us off in a northerly direction, but take it slow. Lance, Dorian, Hicks; you three keep your eyes peeled for anything strange."

Hicks and Lance agreed, but Dorian frowned. He glanced back over his shoulder at the site. He nudged Hicks again.

"Did you ever find anything else in that spot? I mean, any other artifacts?"

"Plenty. But, what specifically?"

Dorian paused. "Physical remains…?"

Hicks shook his head. "None of that."

"I see."

As they ventured further out into the lake, Lance threw a precursory glance toward the sky.

"Uh, I don't like the look of those clouds," he said.

The rest of the team looked up.

"That's strange," said Burke. "They weren't predicting any rain for today."

The sky became dark as black clouds churned, rolled, and expanded. Within seconds the sunny June day was lost to a faux night, requiring them to turn on the Ripley's lights.

Quint glanced up. "Burke! I don't like those clouds."

"They weren't predicting any rain for today," he repeated.

"I don't give a pig's ass who was predicting what! This is my vessel and I'll be damned if we go any further into the most hellish storm I've ever seen."

Burke felt his stomach give out. "But they weren't…" he tried.

No one liked the look of the sky, and no one more so than Dorian. He had been on the ocean many times and been in many nasty storms, some that even seemed determined to wash him and his classmates out to sea. But what he saw gathering above them was a new phenomenon. It was the sort of storm that only comes about every ten, twenty, fifty, or a hundred years or more. Quint was right to call it "hellish". The sky broiled with such malevolence that it seemed as if the apocalypse was upon them. It was like the sky meant to erase them from existence. But there were a couple of characteristics absent from this gathering nightmare that should have been apparent.

"I'm turning this thing around," claimed Quint.

"Wait!" said Dorian. "I know it looks intimidating, but take a closer look. Do you see or hear anything?"

Everyone paused and looked at the sky. After a beat, they turned back to Dorian, bemused.

"There's no lightning or thunder," said Dorian.

They all looked at the sky again, and sure enough, there weren't any lightning bolts streaking across the sky or striking the lake, just as there wasn't any thunder that threatened to destroy their eardrums.

"There's no rain or wind either," added Dorian. "And, the lake itself isn't very choppy. I don't know what *this* is," he said, pointing at the sky, "but it's not a storm."

Hicks looked at him like he had lost his mind. "Look, Dorian, you might be right about all that, but when I look at that sky, I get the heebie-jeebies. The sort of heebie-jeebies that you only get when you feel like your life is about to end. The sort of heebie-jeebies that…" Hicks trailed off and his eyes dimmed with existential dread.

"That what?"

"That I felt when I saw…the Serpent."

Dorian tilted his head to examine Hicks' face. His skin was taut, without character, and his eyes just stared for a thousand miles. He looked ghastly.

"Yeah, man!" piped up Hudson. "I get a feeling I've never had when I look at that sky. A sort of terror I've never felt before—something worse than I've ever imagined!"

"I feel you, man," said Drake.

Burke, however, tried to dismiss all that. "Oh, come, come, come, fellows! As Dorian said, there's no thunder or rain. What could possibly happen? Use your brains. Are you men of science or superstition?"

Drake and Hudson looked equally ashamed, but Lance and Hicks weren't buying it. Quint had his doubts, but hid them beneath a stoic mask.

Dorian looked determined. He knew he should have felt the way Drake and Hudson did, but his gut reaction was more akin to Lance and Hicks'. Despite his fear, though, the storm held answers to the nightmares. He clutched the locket of Cordelia's ashes, and summoned whatever fool's bravery he had left. "Let's stay out for as long as we can. If we hear any rumbling or see any flashes of light, we'll call it a day. Sound reasonable?"

Burke's face lit up. He turned towards the bridge. "What do you say, Quint?"

Quint sighed through his nose. "Very well."

Quint held their bearing, glancing every so often at the darkening sky. It unsettled him in a way few things did. It reminded him of sunken vessels that left their crews to the mercy of the abyss. He shuddered for the first time in many years and tried to forget an incident that took place in the southern Pacific when he was known by another name. Besides the fear he had felt his life, he had also felt a dread deep within his soul. To him, it had always felt like he had come within spitting distance of the devil. He'd never leave his fate in another man's hands. But, now, here he was on one of the world's largest lakes and he could feel that dread again—that gut-wrenching horror that only comes along with the presence of something wholly unnatural and alien. He knew he was on a lake's surface, but for some reason he had the feeling he was piloting a boat on the edge of a void—on top of the veil that separates life from the pale.

Quint couldn't stand the thoughts running through his head. They were foreign to him. He was not a man of fear, and especially not the sort of fear that would result in the loss of sanity should he dwell on it too long. He'd had enough. He was turning the Ripley around; Burke's protests be damned.

"Burke!"

There was no answer.

"Burke!" Quint shouted again.

Again there was no answer.

"Goddamnit, Burke! What the hell are you—?!" Quint turned around, but he stopped when he saw the deck of the Ripley. Every man aboard had fallen unconscious and now littered the deck in various positions. Burke lay in the center of the deck with Drake and Hudson to his left and right, while Hicks lay slumped against the gunwale, Dorian was against the cabin, and Lance had an arm drooped over the gunwale.

"What the…"

Quint slowed the boat and climbed down to the deck. He tried to rouse the others by shaking them and calling their names, but not a single man showed any signs of consciousness. Quint stood over their bodies and felt the pit in his stomach sink even lower. He was filled with an anxiety that as a captain was beyond his worst fears, even worse than those moments of dread he had just experienced looking at the sky. It was his job to make sure every man aboard his vessel survived—from port, out to sea, and back again. It was his responsibility—his duty—to ensure that every man arrived back on land. He checked their vitals and they all seemed to be alive, but none of them were breathing. He couldn't understand how such a thing was possible. He glanced up at the sky as an icy breeze skimmed over his body and he was covered in goose bumps.

"Well…" he tried speaking to himself to calm down. "There's nothing for it. Just have to make it back to shore."

Quint climbed back up to the bridge and turned the Ripley around. He made a heading for south by southeast, and throttled the boat all the way up. He thought he was going in the right direction, but he wasn't sure. He knew for a fact that they hadn't gone that far out, and yet, he could no longer see the shoreline. In every direction he looked, all he could see was the lake and the dismal sky above. The two met on the horizon without the slightest hint of land or civilization beyond. He gripped the wheel with all his might and hoped beyond hope that their new bearing would be their salvation.

***

After Quint's reluctant agreement, Hudson decided that he should get to work. He didn't like looking at the sky, so he thought he would feel safer in the cabin, manning the hydrophone and underwater camera. He put on his headphones and enlarged the feed on the computer connected to the underwater camera. Despite the fact that Lake Superior was supposed to be clear down to twenty-seven feet below the surface, Hudson couldn't see anything of value on the underwater camera, and all he could hear from the hydrophone were the usual underwater noises. He agreed with Dorian on this one—he didn't believe the Serpent could be able to use echolocation. But, then, something started coming through.

It started off as a groan. It was the same sort of sound that a creaky door hinge might make if it was muffled and its cadence was staccato. But that wasn't all. Hudson didn't simply hear it once, but rather the sound was extended and grew in volume. He couldn't explain what he was hearing, but it became weirder when the groan changed pitch and turned into a guttural growl. It was a strange noise that affected Hudson on a primeval level. On one hand, he wanted to continue listening to it because he felt it held some long lost answer about the world, but on the other, he was glad the sound returned to the groan because the growl scared him worse than the clouds.

Hudson continued to listen for another minute as the growl returned for a second or two and then faded out.

A tear streaked from the corner of Hudson's eye, and his body broke out in chills. He'd just realized that he had heard this sound before back when he was working for NOAA. Back in 1997, NOAA recorded an ultra-low-frequency and very powerful sound that they called the "Bloop". They eventually reported that it was the sound of an icequake, but the original story had been much weirder. The original theory was that it had been the sound of a gigantic, aquatic animal—something bigger than a Blue Whale. So, why had he heard it?

That question raised the hair on Hudson's arms. Was this an indication that the icequake story really was just a cover and that it was indeed the sound of a gigantic, aquatic animal? And not just an aquatic animal, but a species of them? No, that couldn't be. The original Bloop was recorded in the southern Pacific Ocean and Hudson was on Lake Superior. Unless that meant there were two varieties of the same species—a freshwater specie and a salt water cousin. Or, it meant that the species could swim in freshwater and salt water, just like a Bull Shark.

But that didn't really matter to Hudson. He was still stuck on the fact that he had heard an exact duplicate of the Bloop in real time. What were the implications of that alone? How many more secrets were being hidden or covered up, and why? What else was a lie?

Hudson watched the feed from the underwater camera, half-expecting to see whatever made the Bloop, but there was nothing there—not even any particles or other kinds of fish. Just water tinted a horrible shade of black from the storm clouds overhead.

Hudson turned away from the camera. He didn't like thinking about the clouds, and he didn't really want to see whatever made the sound. He focused on the hydrophone readings, because while he felt mildly cracked from his experience, he at least knew he wasn't going to lose his mind staring at sound recordings. But, then, he heard something else.

This sound was more normal than the Bloop—it was something that anyone could have heard anywhere…except underwater. It started out as a low wail, almost like the singing of whales from a distance, but this was not a sound that came from a whale. It sounded human, and seemed to contain a sort of melody or rhythm. Against the rest of the silence of the recording, it sent chills up and down his body, his eyes teared up, and a feeling of horror began to rise in his chest.

The wail crescendoed into a scream and before Hudson knew it, he was clutching at his headphones, begging for the noise to stop. He whipped his head from side-to-side, hoping it was his imagination, but the screaming only intensified to a blood-curdling shriek. He went to rip the headphones off when something caught his eye in the underwater camera. There was something far off in the distance—a shape. It was long and serpentine, coiled through the currents. It was more massive than anything he had seen before. Hudson clutched the computer screen and focused his entire attention on what he was seeing. He couldn't believe it—he wouldn't believe it.

As it drew closer, more and more of the creature's body filled the frame until it drew so close that the frame could no longer contain the creature's mass. The creature hardly moved, but when it did, it moved its head almost as if to get a better look at the camera. Soon enough, only its head filled the screen and it appeared as if they were going to hit it. That's when the wail returned, making Hudson's blood run cold, and a glowing red light pierced through the darkness and commanded Hudson's attention.

He saw a flash of something he had never wanted to see, which made something deep within him begin to loosen before reaching a breaking point and shattering. He raised his face and saw the black sky outside the Ripley. He went from looking right in front of him to seeing a thousand miles away. The light of intelligence within his eyes dimmed and never returned.

***

Following Quint's reluctant agreement, Drake got to work. He went back to the cabin and sat opposite Hudson. He checked the sonar's readings on his computer and saw that everything was normal. He sat back and stretched. He looked out the cabin window behind him and at the darkening sky. He shuddered and turned back to his computer, but he couldn't focus as he had become suddenly very sleepy.

Drake slowly opened his eyes and was shocked to find that he had fallen asleep on top of his computer. He sat upright and looked around, wondering why Hudson hadn't woken him. He got his answer immediately as he saw Hudson passed out on his equipment. Drake went around the table and tried to rouse him, but he wouldn't wake up. Drake became anxious and checked his vitals, but his pulse was steady and he was breathing. Still thinking this odd, Drake went out onto the deck and was unprepared for what he found. Everyone else was unconscious as well, including Quint, and the boat had stopped moving. He ran to each one of them, calling their names and shaking them, but none of them would wake up.

Drake looked around and couldn't see anything on the horizon. Had they drifted out into the center of the lake? He looked up at the sky, still covered in black clouds, and he suddenly felt icy cold despite there being no wind.

He ran back into the cabin and picked up the receiver on the radio. He tried to radio an SOS back to Ontonagon or the Coast Guard, but no matter which frequency he tried, he couldn't get a signal. Drake looked around wide-eyed, unsure of what to do. Suddenly, he heard a few beeps. The beeps startled him until he realized they were coming from his computer.

He looked at his monitor and couldn't fathom what the sonar was showing. It told him that there was something out in the lake, but that it appeared to be forty feet long. That was impossible. Though not as impossible as when Drake tried to look back through the recording to see when it started and discovered that the recording had just disappeared. He blinked. He scrolled back to the most recent recording, but it too was gone. He leaned over his computer in complete disbelief.

Drake did the only sensible thing he could think of and restarted his computer. As it booted up, he couldn't help but feel as if he was the only one in the world right now. Everyone else was unconscious, and he couldn't get a signal out. What was going on? He felt like something was toying with him.

He glanced up at the sky and felt a chill in his bones. There were answers in those clouds, but he wasn't sure he wanted them.

His computer finished booting up and he reopened the sonar program, but when he did, he jumped. Somehow the sonar had recorded while the computer was being reset and it showed several masses out in the water at different locations. Some were five to six feet long while others were twenty to fifty feet long. He didn't understand what he was seeing, and further, the computer shouldn't have been able to report anything, so how had it? Drake tried to find a logical explanation, but couldn't come up with one. He decided to err on the side of caution and retrieve the sonar. He'd then go up to the flying bridge and see if he couldn't move Quint and get the Ripley started.

Drake went to the back of the boat. He grabbed the sonar cable and slowly started pulling it up. He fought against the water pressure, but the sonar was coming. It was just about to break the water's surface, when Drake felt a tug. He started for a moment. It had indeed felt like a tug, but what could've done it and why? Deciding he had just lost concentration and dropped it because the cable was wet, he started to retrieve it again, but there was another tug.

Drake started to lose his composure and a part of him just wanted to leave the sonar in the lake for now, but another part of him reasoned that it was an expensive bit of equipment and if something did indeed have it, he would fight to keep it.

Drake widened his posture and bent his knees. He latched onto the cable as tightly as he could and pulled, but something fought back. He put more force into his pull and strained, but something stronger than him returned the favor, and before he could react, Drake found himself pulled into the lake.

He broke the surface and gasped. He reached out for the Ripley's gunwale, but something pulled him down by the ankle. As if that wasn't terrifying enough, Drake had had the sensation that it was a hand. He pulled his leg away and tried for the gunwale again, but this time, something that felt like an arm wrapped around his neck and pulled him into the dark water below.

Drake forced his eyes open and looked for what had pulled him under, but the water was too dark for him to see anything farther than his reach. He trod the water for a minute before deciding to go back up to the surface for air, but when he did, he was shocked to see that the Ripley had disappeared. He twisted every which way, looking for the boat, but couldn't find it. A pit developed in his chest and descended down to his gut as chills raced up and down his body. What sort of nightmare was he having?

He felt someone dragging him down again. Beyond irritated with this strange experience, he pulled his leg up and pushed his face beneath the surface, but immediately wished he hadn't. He saw a face, but couldn't make it out. Was it the face of someone who drowned, someone who burned to death, or someone who was hanged? All three were just as likely as they were unlikely, but one thing that was definite was that the person was dead.

Drake pulled his face out of the water, and when he did, he saw something just beyond the still water. Something was sitting on the surface. It was gigantic with black skin and a serpent's body, but it was too far to make out any details. Drake didn't need the details however as he felt a primal desire to get away from it. He turned as fast as he could and tried to throw himself forward. He knew there was nowhere to go, but anywhere was better than here. But, as he threw himself, his head collided into something hard that knocked him senseless. He slipped beneath the surface and as his vision darkened, he saw the outline of the bottom of the Ripley and his free-floating sonar.

Back on the boat, Hicks' eyes opened a sliver and he groaned, "Draaaaa…?"

Dorian spasmed and chirped, "—ake."

***

Lance knew the dark clouds were ominous and that they shouldn't be out there, but he didn't feel like he was in danger until Quint agreed to Dorian's plan. The fact that they had made a reasonable decision about something so unreasonable was rejected by the totality of his being. If he hadn't been on a boat out in the middle of a lake, he would've run the other way as fast as he could. The whole plan was insane. But the panic he faced at their decision was nothing compared to the sheer terror he faced as he watched Dorian, Burke, and Hicks all fall to the deck floor unconscious. He tried to help them, but he too was conquered by a supernatural drowsiness. The last thing he remembered was stumbling toward the gunwale before passing out on it.

Lance opened his eyes and discovered that he was in a tent. For a minute, nothing made sense. He rose and looked around. Inside the tent, he saw all his camping gear. Not the camping gear he currently had, but the camping gear he'd had when he was a boy. Was this a dream? Or was being on Lake Superior with six other men when he was an old man a dream?

He got out of his sleeping bag and exited the tent to an awaiting campfire. There was a man sitting next to it on a rock, grilling fish. The man smiled.

"Morning, boy! Sleep well?"

"Dad?!"

Lance paused. Seeing his father alive and well wasn't the only weird thing about this. When he had spoken, he hadn't recognized his voice. It sounded like a child's. He looked down at his hands, and saw the fresh, taut skin of youth. He touched his face and instead of feeling wrinkles, he felt smooth skin with no evidence of stubble and a slight plumpness to his cheeks. He grabbed a handful of his hair and instead of it being sparse and dry, it was lush and thick. He looked at his father, awestruck.

"Something the matter, son?"

"It's just…I thought I was an old man."

His father chuckled. "Not for many years yet, boy! It must've been a dream you had."

"Must have… It seemed so real, though. I was on a boat out in the middle of Lake Superior with…"

"With what? Or who?"

"…I can't remember. I do remember feeling scared, though. And not like any kind of scared I've been before. Like, I feared for my life. Or rather, I feared for my soul. I had the feeling I was standing upon the precipice of eternal damnation, and there wasn't anything I could do to escape it."

His father was silent for a minute before snickering again. "Hoo, boy! What a vocabulary you got. No wonder you're smarter than your old man."

Lance was confused. It seemed like his father, but it also didn't seem like his father. If Lance had used language like that when he was ten, shouldn't his father have scolded him for "damnation" and told him not to worry, that it was just a dream?

"Eat up, boy! We've got to hit the trail before the sun gets too high. We don't want to be ascending the Porkies with the sun at its summit. We definitely want to be descending."

Lance nodded and started preparing for his day. He was sure to eat, dress, and get all his hiking gear together, but when he found himself and his father half way up the trail in a blink of an eye, he didn't remember doing any that. He must have, though, because how else could he have gotten to this point? But then it dawned on him that he didn't remember the way they had come. The panic started to grow as he realized that if he needed to, he couldn't find the way back to their camp on his own.

"Dad! I don't remember the trail!"

"Hm? What's that, now?"

"I don't remember how we got out here!"

"So?"

"So?!"

Lance couldn't believe what he'd heard. His father was a great trailblazer and tracker, and he had taught Lance well from a young age how to do the same. In fact, it was often his father's pleasure to lead them deep into the woods and then test Lance's hiking skills by telling him to lead them back to camp.

Lance looked helplessly at his father. "What if—!"

"Never mind, son. I remember the trail. We'll be fine. I'm not going to test you on it anyway. This is your vacation—not a survival exercise."

That sounded reasonable to Lance, but the situation seemed unreasonable. Lance blinked. Why did that thought seem so familiar and terrifying?

"Come, boy! Not long to go yet!"

Lance followed his father through a section of trail that he somehow remembered, which was odd because this should've been his first time in this part of the Porkies. And yet, the trees and underbrush all looked similar. He even accurately predicted the moment a hawk was going to fly overhead, but unlike last time, his father didn't point it out.

Last time?

The scene in front of Lance seemed to spasm and this time, his father pointed out the hawk, just like he was supposed to. "Look, boy! A hawk! Noble creature!"

They continued on and at a point in the trail where his father was supposed to turn right, he turned left. Lance looked down the trail where they were supposed to go and saw another man and child headed down that trail. Lance recognized the man as his father and the child as himself. His father even stopped to point something out to the other Lance. Lance remembered all of that, but when he turned to face his father, there was no interaction at all. Was he getting premonitions of the future, or was he seeing multiple realities within his region of time and space, like he had seen from that special on TV?

"Dad? Are you sure this is the right—"

Lance stopped when he and his father came to a clearing near the edge of the lake. From a tree were six persons, all hanged, and the forest around them was roaring with flames. Lance turned and saw that the spot where they were was nothing but fire now. He could feel the heat scorch his skin and he retreated until he bumped into his father, who looked down at him with no emotion.

"This isn't how it's supposed to go!" Lance cried out.

"It isn't?" his father asked. "What about this?"

The scene changed. The fire was gone as were the bodies and they were on a different edge of the lake. Behind his father, Lance could see someone swimming when suddenly, something caught them. They struggled against it and tried to pull their leg away, but whatever had them wouldn't let go. The person fought and fought, but they were soon exhausted. They called for help.

Lance took a step in the direction of the lake, but noticed his father's face. Again, there was no reaction.

"We should help…"

But his father didn't move. Instead, he said, "This isn't right either, is it?"

Lance shook. "No…it isn't."

The scene changed again. They were back to the burning forest, but Lance's father had disappeared. He looked around, but didn't see him. The forest flames threatened to consume him, so he took a few steps away, but bumped into something that moved when he hit it. He turned around and saw that it was a hanging body. He looked up into the face and recognized it as his father. Lance screamed.

He broke down and started wailing on the ground. Tears drenched his face and mucous saturated his lips. He cried harder than he ever had in his life. He couldn't believe it.

"No, Dad! No! This can't be! This isn't real!"

"You mean…this isn't right?"

Lance stopped crying and his eyes widened. He looked up at his father once again and saw the expressionless face.

Lance stood up and took several steps away. "What the hell…?"

The scene changed again. Lance was back on the bank, but he was alone. He looked for his father, but his mind realized the awful truth before his eyes could process what he was about to see. He looked out at the drowning swimmer and saw his father there, waving an arm, hoping to be rescued. Lance charged toward the water's surface, but stopped short. His father yet again had the expressionless face.

Lance clutched his head and fell to the ground. He couldn't process what was happening. What was he seeing? Why was it happening? How could he escape it? He felt like his mind was going to tear itself in half. If this nightmare didn't end soon, he was sure he was going to go mad. Panic and fear swirled within him, creating a vortex within his body that he could feel go higher and higher. When it reached his brain, he knew he was done for.

"This isn't right, either?" said his father's voice.

"No! None of this is right! This isn't the vacation we had! None of this is in my memories!"

"Rue life, disdain memory—"

"What?!"

"—the dead belong with the dead…"

"What?! Dad! I don't understand! Why is this happening?"

"Why?" his father responded. "Eyes of the dead conspire against the living," he replied in a voice different from his own.

Tears resumed their trail down Lance's face. "I-I still don't…"

"Fear welcomes all, death accepts all fearful—to fear is to die—the Serpent is death."

"The Serpent?!"

Lance had a vision. He saw his arm as it hung over a gunwale on a boat out in the middle of a lake. The scene was dark as if it was night.

"To live with memory is torture—to die to memory is solace, the Serpent is salvation."

"I don't understand!" Lance screamed at the top of his lungs. "Just tell me how to end this nightmare!" he whimpered.

"Very well," his father said. "We are prisoners of the creature of the lake. It controls these waters and all who cross them. Once you venture out onto them, you are doomed to its will."

As Lance's father spoke, the scene changed multiple times. One minute the forest was on fire with six dead bodies hanging from a tree and his father in front of him to them being on the bank, staring at a swimmer drown.

"There is only one way to end this nightmare. We have to die in this dream."

During that speech, the scene had flashed again to Lance's father hanging in the tree to drowning in the lake. And the scene continued to flash between those four as the conversation continued. Lance kept his eyes on his father's and absorbed every word for desperation had robbed him of his senses, though somewhere in the back of his mind, there was a voice screaming a question. It wanted to know when his father's eyes had turned red.

"Die?!" replied Lance. "Dad! I don't think I can do that."

"You can, boy. I believe in you. You can do anything you set your mind to."

"Dad! This isn't the same. This isn't like climbing a tree or finding my way back to camp. You're asking me to die in a dream to escape it! How can I…?"

"This is no different from those experiences. It's just that instead of finding your way back to camp, you're finding your way out of this. You want out, don't you?"

More tears streamed down his face. Lance clutched his hair and screamed out of frustration. He wailed as hard as he could and threw a tantrum against the ground.

"You're my dad! How could you do this to me?! How?!"

"I'm sorry, boy," he said with a slight tinge of sadness. "But, this is the only way. Grab the rope there and climb the tree. Tie it to the tree and then around your neck, and just fall. I promise you that all of this will end when your neck breaks."

Lance bawled all the more. It was his last defense against the unreasonable demands of his father. But like a child who knows he can't disobey, he stood robotically and grabbed the rope. Despite the fact that he saw grass, it felt like hard wood. And with the tears still streaming, his silent petition for an answer that was anything but this, he proceeded to climb the tree. His hands reached out and every so often, he saw the hands of an old man, grasping a ladder.

Lance made it to the top of the tree where he tied the rope around the branch and then looped it around his neck. He looked down at his father, who while still hanging, was now hanging above a lake.

Lance sniffled. "You promise…?" he whined. "You promise this dream will end after I jump."

"I promise."

Lance sniffled one last time, mustered up his courage, and stepped off the branch. As he fell, the forest fell away to a lake and the tree became a boat. Lance realized his horrible mistake at the last second and tried to find something to grab onto, but as he looked up to the dark clouds in the sky, he felt the noose tighten, his body pulled, stopped, and tugged, and the pressure in his neck gave way with one savage crack and before the pain could register, Lance Fox was dead.

***

Burke gave an enthusiastic nod to Dorian when Quint granted their condition. He was pleased that their expedition wouldn't be derailed by something so trivial as a few dark clouds. He had seen plenty of cloudy days without rain in his time.

He began to rummage around in their gear, looking for a camera, when the drowsiness struck. It was sudden and merciless. Burke couldn't imagine why he felt so sleepy, and even the effort of trying to think that much was an astounding burden. He stumbled and fell somewhere in the center of the deck, but he couldn't care as sleep enveloped him.

Burke blinked. He found himself standing in a lush forest. He didn't know how he got there, but he did know that he had a deadline. He had to photograph a pack of wild wolves and send the pictures to his editor by this afternoon. He delved deeper into the woods, walking as quietly as he could so he didn't startle anything. He never knew what sort of opportunity was going to present itself, but if he should see a bear, coyote, or cougar, he knew he could make some money off them. But it wasn't really the money that drove Burke to become a wildlife photographer—it had been the pleasure. He loved animals and being out in nature. How could anyone not?

Burke blinked again and found himself on a trail he recognized, but he didn't know why. He knew this was his first time here. But what was stranger was how quickly he proceeded down the trail every time he blinked. Before he knew it, he came to a clearing with a downed tree, and just beyond it, the area in which a pack of wolves lived. He crouched down and headed for the fallen tree. When he was within fifty feet of it, he crawled on his belly until he was right behind it and readied his camera. He lifted his head above the trunk and could just make out a few wolfish heads. He brought up his camera and waited.

The wolves came closer and inspected the horizon. Burke could tell they knew he was there, but he hoped they knew he wasn't dangerous and wouldn't leave. But then there was a bright flash of light in the sky. The wolves looked up, their pupils contracted, and they fled in an instant. Burke was likewise startled and looked into the sky.

Something was etched across the blue sky. It was long—Burke couldn't say how long as he didn't know how high up it was, but it made him feel tiny in comparison. The entity gave off a dazzling, white light that made the sun look dim. Burke stared at it. He was mesmerized. Despite its immense size and odd brightness, the thing didn't scare him, but filled him with a great sense of wonder and childlike awe. It was like seeing a dragon, and that's what Burke thought it was for a second. It was serpentine and seemed to have wing-like protrusions from its center mass that dazzled on their own, but other than those two characteristics, there was nothing draconic about it. It might have been a phoenix instead. Whatever it was, it was beautiful, and Burke felt like his mind was open for the first time in his life.

Burke lifted his camera to the sky and snapped as many pictures as he could. The creature continued tracing the sky until it flew out of sight. Burke let his camera fall to his chest, and he reveled in the ecstasy of his discovery. This was the single most important moment of his life, and while he knew that, he didn't understand the lingering consequences of this moment.

He went home and uploaded the shots of the creature to his computer. They were majestic, but ultimately failed to capture the true beauty of the creature. He was both elated and disappointed. If only he could see it one more time...

Over the next few weeks, Burke set to work trying to figure out what the creature was. He sent copies of the photograph to his editor and every other wildlife photographer he knew. They were all equally puzzled about the pictures, but they were also deeply troubled. Something about the images didn't sit right with them. They had all promised themselves not to say anything to Burke about it, but then he became completely obsessed about it. The creature was all he talked about and he was determined to figure out what it was. He revisited the same site over and over again, hoping to see it, but day after day, week after week, and month after month, the entity never showed itself again. But this lack of luck did not dissuade Burke.

Burke kept pushing. He insisted that this creature existed. He contacted everyone and anyone he could to prove its existence. He even submitted the photo to his local news station looking for other eyewitnesses. He posted the photo on the Internet, but no one came forward. What was worse was that one by one, people started to turn on Burke. The best of them just stopped contacting him, but with others, the backlash was more severe. Burke was slandered as a fraud, and not only were the photos labeled as fake, but all the pictures he had taken of extant animals were also subjected to scrutiny. There were those who claimed he stole work from others or copied them. He was criticized for sub-standard efforts, and little by little, Burke felt like he was going mad.

At the time of his sighting, he had felt a great thrill. He had seen something truly beautiful and he had only wanted to share it with the world and learn all he could about it. But, now, it had cost him everything. He lost all his friends, his colleagues ridiculed him, his contacts and customers black listed him, and his bank account was beginning to run dry.

It all came to a head. Burke couldn't take it anymore. His reputation was in ruins and his finances were stretched. He had lost sleep over all the stress. He stared at himself in his bedroom mirror with dark circles under his red eyes. He was exhausted and on the verge of tears. He looked like a mad man. All he had to do was end it by denying the existence of the creature. He looked at himself in the mirror and clenched his fists. "It's... It's not... It's not r—"

Burke looked at the corner of his mirror where he had taped the best picture of the beast. Although the picture didn't do its sparkling form justice, it was enough to ignite a fire within Burke and renew the memory in his head. He closed his eyes and saw the creature blaze across the sky.

"It's not re—It's not r—It's not—It's not—It's—It's not—Goddamnit!"

Burke collapsed to the floor. He couldn't do it. He couldn't deny the existence of the creature. He wasn't man enough to lie to himself. He knew what he saw when he saw it. It *had* to be real, but what was it? Where had it gone? And why hadn't anyone else heard of it? Burke was beyond frustrated, but he was desperate for answers, so once again, he turned to his computer and continued to search.

He must've been at it for hours. In time, exhaustion won out and sleep claimed him. He fell asleep at his desk and didn't wake up until a few hours later when an alert went off on his computer. He looked at the screen and checked the alert. It was his email. He didn't know the sender, but in the subject line, they said they believed him. He was weary of opening it as he had received several emails from people claiming to believe him only to make fun of him. But as he read this message, it seemed genuine. The sender identified himself as a "cryptozoologist"—one who studies undocumented animals, and while he had never seen the creature Burke took a photo of, he had examined all the pictures and concluded that the creature was real.

This was the start of something new for Burke. A whole new world of mystery and intrigue opened up to him when he accepted the fact that there could still be animals out in the world not documented. To some, it seemed like a long shot and a deep, meandering path towards further obscurity, but Burke took the plunge. He sold off anything he didn't need, including his house, and bought a van. With it, he traveled the country, stopping anywhere where something unknown had been seen. He took his cameras and utilizing his knowledge as a wildlife photographer, he tracked his query. He made new friends and colleagues along the way, people who actually gave him the time of day, who looked at his glaring, sky dragon, and tried to make sense of it. In exchange, he went on expeditions with them, documenting the whole journey along the way. He had taken several interesting shots, but nothing conclusive. However, his new experiences had turned him into an "expert" and after writing a few self-published books and being interviewed for a few shows and podcasts, his life and well-being slowly started to return. In time, he could afford to buy a new house and re-establish his career, but the journey for the truth was not an easy one, especially when weathered for years.

It had been more than a decade since he took the pictures of the light dragon. He had been back to the site with his new cryptozoologist and paranormal investigator friends. He had taken ufologists, astrophysicists, geologists, astronomers, psychics, witches, shamans, and New Age practitioners and told them his amazing story, and every new person had a new theory, but none of them resonated with him. He listened to their theories, no matter how mundane or how crazy. He'd nod and say, "That's interesting," but after every interview, he'd slink back to his van, bed, or home, and refute everything they had said. He maintained that it was a living, breathing creature. And the fact that he had not seen it again or heard of it again weighed upon his morale like lead. How long could he continue the search? How long could he look for something that he was starting to believe he would never see again?

That's why Burke had jumped at the opportunity to investigate the Superior Serpent. Hicks had sent him a message and he replied. Hicks' creature was a lake serpent and scared him half to death, but it resonated with Burke in that it was too unbelievable. Forests full of wild men, wolves walking on their hind legs, men who looked like moths flying around TNT factories, and gargoyles that drank goat's blood; those all had a certain appeal about them. They had been seen by enough eyewitnesses that they could be real, but Burke's dragon had only been seen by him and it sounded like Hicks' serpent had only been seen by him, too. At least, that's how it seemed at first. After Hicks' story went public, reports came rolling in about the creature, but Burke was already committed to the project. He couldn't back out now, but there was still a chance the Serpent might lead to the dragon. There was still a chance…

"How long can you run on blind hope?" said a voice.

"Who are you?" asked Burke.

"I'm you, moron."

Burke's memories of the past few years disappeared and everything went dark. Someone that looked like him appeared, except this version of him was cloaked in shadow and wore a perpetual scowl.

"You've searched and searched all these years. You've listened to experts far and wide, but you've never come across anything concrete. How can you be sure you saw what you saw?"

"Because I know what I saw."

"Maybe you had a stroke. You ever think of that?"

"Who *are* you?!"

"Weren't you listening?" said the shadow Burke. "I'm you."

"No, you can't be."

"Alright, fine. You're right. I'm not *you*. I'm the you that you've been keeping hidden all these years. I'm the resentment and anger you squirreled away when your sanity was first called into question. I'm the rebuttal you've always felt any time you couldn't accept a new theory about the creature. I'm the part of you that is sick and tired of this wandering and searching bullshit! I don't care about the creature anymore. It has only brought me misery and doubt. It was a demon in angel's light!"

"That's not true. I felt great wonder at seeing it the first time!"

"The same 'wonder' you felt at seeing a couple of blurry Bigfoot photos that could've easily been shadows or a tree stump? The same 'wonder' you felt at hearing audio of a few unknown howls that could've been caused by faulty equipment? The same 'wonder' that led you to believe you thought you saw something swooping in the night sky over Pointe Pleasant or something bouncing around in the shadows of San Juan?!

"Admit it! You've never seen anything that you actually believe exists. You've never seen anything that convinces you that these things exist, and even *you* have admitted to yourself more than once that what you saw could've been a glare on your glasses."

"No, it couldn't have been. I have pictures!"

"Pictures taken with a camera pointed up at the sky tilted towards the sun!"

"I saw it move! It flew across the sky!"

"And now, I can feel all the resentment you have toward this expedition. You were excited when you found out about a 'unique' cryptid. Maybe the two were connected, or distantly related. Were you really so naïve?!"

"I don't see anything wrong with being hopeful," replied Burke. "It has kept my spirits high no matter what happens."

"And forced you to lie to yourself about what's actually happening around you. 'Silver lining' my ass. You lie to yourself to shelter yourself from your disappointment, just as you're lying to yourself now. You're disappointed that no one is actually committed to finding the Serpent. They're only here for the money. Even Hicks took some convincing as he wasn't that interested in the truth. He was just looking for people to commiserate with, to know that he wasn't crazy, which is exactly what you've never found.

"No one but you has seen the dragon of light. No one but you knows the burden of knowing it exists. No one has any proof of this creature that has completely ruined your reputation and cost you your friends. But, look what happens the second you head out onto the lake to look for Hicks' sea serpent—the sky becomes possessed and every man aboard this vessel goes through his own hell. Hicks' serpent exists, but yours does not. And you hate him all the more for it!"

Burke's world shattered. While there were things spoken by his shadow self that were outright lies, there was some truth. Burke had lied to himself about always looking for a silver lining. He had lied to himself about being a positive person. In reality, he wanted nothing more than to be validated for his sighting, for the creature he saw to be proven real, but it would never happen. And now, here he was looking for an even more bewildering creature and it appeared to be real. And he hated the creature and everyone who had seen it for that fact. This was real—his experience years ago may not have been.

And Burke *hated* them all for that.

***

After Quint agreed to Dorian's terms, Dorian himself felt overcome by exhaustion. He didn't know the origin of the spell, but not wishing to make a spectacle of himself, he leaned back against the cabin wall and watched everyone else as they worked. He folded his arms and looked up at the sky. The foreboding clouds sent shivers down his spine and with each succeeding shiver, his drowsiness grew. His eyes half closed. He felt like he was falling, but didn't know why until his butt collided with the deck of the Ripley. That's what he deduced anyway as he couldn't really see anything, and further, he didn't care as he slipped into sleep.

Dorian had no idea how long he slept, but he did wake up shivering. He looked up and instead of seeing the ominous clouds, he saw the night sky. He nearly panicked at the implications, until he realized he seemed to be the only one on the boat. No one else was around, and for some reason, his legs wouldn't let him stand up.

"You've been asleep for a while," said a voice that left Dorian breathless.

He looked up and saw Cordelia standing before him. She smiled at him and squat down, wrapping her arms around her knees.

"Is it really you?!"

Cordelia looked down.

"Is this real?"

"It is and it isn't," she said. "This is just a dream, but I am really here."

"H-How?"

"I'm dead. Remember?"

"So, you can infiltrate my dreams?"

"Only under certain circumstances. Only when you're connected to *it*."

"It?"

Cordelia shivered. "The…*beast*. The *creature*. The thing you're looking for."

Dorian paused. "I don't understand. How am I connected to it?"

"You're on the lake. This is its domain. I mean, it's not in the physical realm, but it still holds all the power here. Its servants control everything here while it remains trapped."

"I still don't understand…"

"Never mind," said Cordelia, standing. "That's not why I'm here. I came to tell you that you need to leave. It wants you all dead. In fact, it's already killed two of your crew."

Dorian felt a chill go through his body. He saw a transparent man walk to the back of the boat and fall off. He then saw a second climb up to the bridge.

"Drake? Lance?! They're dead?!"

Cordelia nodded. "It won't be satisfied until you all are. That's what it does. It kills and collects the souls of the dead. It's a demon. It will harbor them until the end of time." Cordelia looked sad.

Dorian stared at her for a second before realizing. "Wait! Does that mean it will harbor you until the end of time?"

Cordelia looked away.

"Cordelia! Answer me!"

"You're not responsible for saving me."

"How can you say that?! I have to do something!"

"No! You stay and it will only kill and capture you, too. I want you to go on living. I want you to find another girl and love her like you loved me. Show her everything she was missing from her life."

"No! I can't! I can't live without you!"

"You must." Cordelia leaned down and grabbed the locket that contained her ashes.

"What are you doing?"

Cordelia turned toward the lake and threw the locket into the water. Dorian couldn't move to stop her.

"You have to move on," she said. "This is where I belong. 'The dead belong with the dead'—at least that much is true." Cordelia smiled at him. "Thank you for everything."

Dorian's will to stand, to take hold of Cordelia and wrap her in his arms, to seize her and never let go, broke through the spell that had put him to sleep, and he dragged himself out of the dream. He forced his eyes open, and with a snarl, he stood up, only to find that Cordelia had disappeared. He no longer saw her, and instead he stood back on the Ripley with everyone else.

Dorian roared his frustration up to the darkened heavens and collapsed back on his knees. He began sobbing, and as he often did when he needed some comfort, he reached for the locket of Cordelia's ashes. But as he felt around his chest, groping for them, he couldn't find them. Dorian's eyes went wide and he looked down at his chest as he scratched away at his shirt and neck. The locket was gone. He stood up to the gunwale and looked out into the water as tears streamed down his face.

***

Hicks was on the flying bridge, trying to bring Lance's body back on the boat when he heard commotion from below. He looked and saw Dorian standing. That was a bit of good news. He had tried to rouse him, but like the others, Hicks couldn't wake him. Hicks was relieved to see him awake until he started screaming at the open water and collapsed. He then watched as Dorian cried, felt around his chest, then scratched at it panic-stricken, before standing and looking out over the lake. What had happened to him?

"Dorian," he called from the flying bridge. "Dorian! Are you all right?"

Dorian slowly turned to face him. Hicks recoiled to see the tears streaming down his face.

"My God, man. What happened to you?"

Dorian turned back toward the lake. He sniffled. "She's gone, Hicks. She's gone…"

"Who?"

"Cordelia."

"Who?" Hicks' eyes darted down to Dorian's chest and saw that the golden locket from around his neck was gone. He hadn't asked about it, but he had had the inkling that it held something precious to Dorian. He put some of the pieces together.

"You're…girlfriend? Wasn't she already 'gone'?"

"No. Before she was only dead. And she was always with me, but now she's gone for good. A prisoner of this goddamned lake!"

"What're you talking about?"

Dorian muttered for a few seconds, trying to get words out. Finally, he said, "Hicks…what the hell happened to us?"

"A very good question," replied Hicks. He shivered as a breeze blew. "From what I can tell, after the clouds rolled in, we all passed out. I remember feeling drowsy immediately after Drake and Hudson went into the cabin. I passed out somewhere along the stern and on the gunwale. And then…I felt something that nearly scared the shit out of me.

"Although, I wasn't completely conscious of it as I drifted in and out of consciousness, sleeping for several hours at a time—I know because I remember seeing the night sky occasionally in breaks in the clouds—but I felt that absolute terror and dread that I did when the clouds rolled in. It was the same dread and terror I felt when I first saw the Serpent. And it was right there somewhere," said Hicks, pointing to the lake right next to the rear corner of the boat. "It sat there and waited like a predator waiting to pounce, but I never let my guard down. I never let it in my brain. I could feel it, and I knew that if I surrendered my defenses, it would get me.

"I even remember at some point or another briefly catching a glimpse of Drake's head and then hearing a splash behind me. I later heard a thud and…well, I can't find him aboard. He's not in the cabin, the head, or anywhere. I think he's…dead."

Dorian nodded. He wiped some of the tears away from his face. "He is indeed."

Hicks grimaced. "The next thing I remember after that is seeing Lance out of the corner of my eye as he climbed up to the bridge, and then I was completely helpless to stop him from…"

Hicks and Dorian turned toward the port side of the Ripley. Lance still hung there, the shock and horror of what he did and tried to stop still on his face.

"I don't know what was going through his mind," continued Hicks, "but from what I remember, it looked as if he realized too late that he was making a mistake.

"As for everyone else, I haven't been able to wake them. I only woke up myself about ten minutes ago. I don't know how or why, but the drowsiness that claimed me finally wore off and I was able to think again. What got me back on my feet was hearing Lance's body bounce off the side of the boat."

Dorian looked at the lake and thought back to what Cordelia had said. "We need to get off this lake," he said with some semblance of his former self.

"You don't need to tell me twice," replied Hicks. "But, I don't know how to do that. Quint doesn't have a life boat, and I'm not trusting my life to a life jacket. Whatever got Drake must still be out there. I would start the boat myself, but Quint is all over the controls. And we really should do something about Lance."

"We should," agreed Dorian.

He climbed up to the flying bridge and helped Hicks bring him back onto it. They decided to cover him with a blanket and leave him there for the time being. Struggling to get him off the bridge didn't seem like a smart thing to do with only the two of them awake.

"What now?" asked Hicks.

Dorian considered their options, and realized they didn't have many. "The only thing we can do is to try and slide Quint away from the wheel and see if we can't get the boat started."

"Right…"

Hicks and Dorian looked at each other before stepping to either side of Quint. They each grabbed a handful of wrist and shoulder, and prepared to move him back, but to their surprise, Quint's shocked expression met their faces.

"What the hell?!"

"Quint?!"

They both jumped back.

"What're you two up to?! What the hell's going on? Where are we?" Quint stood up and looked out over the lake and up to the sky. He looked more bewildered than they did. "What's going on?" he asked once more.

Hicks and Dorian explained what they were trying to do. Quint furrowed his brow at first and then looked concerned.

"You mean to tell me I was out?"

"Yeah," said Dorian with a shrug.

"Sonuva bitch! I thought I was awake! I thought I was looking for shore! What the hell happened?!"

Hicks explained what he thought had happened based on what he found when he woke up. Quint's expression became all the more alarmed, especially when he looked over at Lance's body.

"Jesus Christ! And you mean to tell me Drake's dead, too?!"

"We're pretty sure he is," replied Dorian.

"Dammit, man! We can't settle for 'pretty sure'. We have to be absolutely sure. Sound the alarm! Man overboard! Get some of these damned searchlights on! And see what you can do about Burke and Hudson. I'm going to get the boat started."

Hicks ran around the boat turning on the searchlights as Quint got the Ripley started. The roar of its engines was pleasantly mundane. It reminded them that they were still on Earth. Dorian meanwhile went over to Burke to wake him. He however didn't need to. Burke had actually been awake since

Hicks' and Dorian's first conversation. He was playing possum, hoping to glean some useful information. He pretended to be startled when Dorian placed his hand on him.

"Ah! Dorian! What's going on?!"

"Some serious shit. Hicks will explain later."

"Are we still on the lake or are we in port?"

"We're on the lake still. And we may be yet for some time. Quint insists on looking for Drake. We think he fell overboard."

"Oh, I see."

"You sit tight. I'm going to go see about Hudson."

"Good idea," replied Burke. He had no problem with staying out of the way while he watched the lesser beings scuttle around the boat, minding the mundane. He would watch and wait. He would get them for this and prove the experience as real in hopes of returning some shred of dignity to his life.

Dorian went into the cabin and jumped back when he saw Hudson's head up. He was staring out the window with his mouth open. Dorian was startled, but relieved to see that Hudson was awake.

"Hudson?" he said, placing a hand on his shoulder, but Hudson didn't respond. "Hudson!" Dorian gave him a shake.

Hudson finally turned to face Dorian, but did so so slowly that Dorian felt chills throughout his entire body. When Hudson's eyes locked with his, he could tell something was off. While Hudson was looking at him, he wasn't focused on him. He was looking through Dorian and beyond.

Dorian knelt down to Hudson's level. "What in God's name happened to you?"

Hudson turned back to the window and continued to stare up at the sky. Drool began to drip down the corner of his mouth.

Dorian ran back outside and hurried up to the bridge. "We've got another problem!"

"Oh, no," said Hicks.

"What now?" said Quint as he brought the boat around and started heading south.

"Hudson's lost his mind."

"What?!" said both Quint and Hicks.

"I don't know how or why, but I'm pretty sure he's insane."

"That's bullshit!" said Quint. "Dorian, take the wheel."

Dorian did so as Quint and Hicks rushed down to the cabin.

"Hudson! Hudson!" called Quint. "Goddammit, when I call your name, you look at me! Hudson!"

"Come on, buddy," said Hicks from his other side. "Don't do this to us."

Hudson didn't respond to either of them despite being yelled and cursed at and shaken by Quint.

"Dammit, Hudson! Don't make me clock you one!"

"Quint," said an even voice from behind him.

Quint turned and almost jumped to see Burke. He hadn't recognized the tone of voice.

"That won't do him any good. We'll just have to take him to a hospital when we get to shore. Leave him with me. You two continue the search for Drake. But, honestly, I wouldn't bother."

"What?!"

Quint and Hicks were both beyond disbelief to hear Burke speak that way.

"With a dead man aboard and another out of his mind, our priority should be getting back to shore. The Coast Guard can look for Drake."

"Fuck me!" said Quint. "And fuck you, Burke! The Coast Guard will be six hours too fucking late to find Drake if we report it. He'll be dead long before then!"

"He's probably dead now."

"Then looking for him now won't do him or us anymore harm!" Quint pushed past Burke and stormed out.

"He didn't mean it, Burke," quelled Hicks.

"I know. He's just frustrated and stressed. We'll sort this out eventually, but everyone's a little scared right now. It's okay. We're entitled to be after what happened."

"Exactly," agreed Hicks. He left the cabin placated as Burke had sounded reasonable, but his voice was lacking its usual affability. Something about the whole conversation sent chills through his body.

When they were alone, Burke turned toward Hudson. "Alright, you spineless shit," he whispered. "What did you see that made you cuckoo?"

Hudson didn't respond, but as Burke leaned closer, something on Hudson's computer screens caught his attention. They both displayed recordings of several hours. What had he seen? Burke helped himself to Hudson's headphones and started scanning through the audio and camera recordings.

***

For hours they scanned the top of Lake Superior for any sign of Drake. They shouted his name over the water and splashed light all over the surface. Every second that ticked away added more and more doubt to Quint's mind and more and more assurance to Hicks' and Dorian's. They knew he was gone, but they went with the search as it was important to Quint. It might have even been his way of grieving. And as captain, he felt responsible. Aboard his vessel he ruled and acted as God.

This all was fine with Burke as he pored through Hudson's computers. He had found the audio and visual evidence almost immediately since they were near the start of the recordings. He heard the call of the Serpent and saw its shadowy form on the camera, but neither its form nor its call made him go mad for he already was. Most of his time was spent searching the rest of the video and the audio, but nothing else interesting showed up. He contemplated what to do with the files. With them, he could finally prove he wasn't crazy, but what would happen if the others saw and heard them? Would they go crazy too or would they remain sane and insist on their destruction as they had left Hudson barely more than comatose?

As Burke considered what to do, he got curious and checked Drake's computer too, but the apparent malfunctions that had lured him into the water hadn't been recorded. Burke didn't know all that, so all he could do was speculate on why or how Drake's computer was empty of evidence whereas Hudson's had it all. The two should have recorded phenomena at the exact same times and yet they hadn't. Perhaps there was something physical to the phenomena on Hudson's computers, but wholly supernatural on Drake's. Or maybe sonar wasn't any good on picking up spiritual matter. After all, video recordings, photographs, and audio recordings of ghosts did exist, but because they weren't physical, maybe sonar didn't bounce off them. It was an odd theory, but the silver lining meant that Burke only had to tamper with Hudson's files and not Drake's, meaning he would leave less evidence behind in case the others caught onto him. With that in mind, Burke began disconnecting the external hard drives that had collected the recordings, when Hicks appeared in the doorway.

"Burke?"

Burke jumped. "What?!" he said tense.

"We can't find any sign of Drake."

"I see…"

"But, the good news is that day is beginning to break and the ominous clouds above are dissipating. Quint says we're heading back."

"Very well."

Hicks looked at Burke's hands. "Are those Hudson's drives?"

"They are."

"Do you think he recorded whatever it was that made him lose his mind?"

"Ah, I had the same thought. I've been trolling through the footage and audio files, but I couldn't find anything."

"Damn," said Hicks, his shoulders dropping. "Well, that's what's going on."

"Okay."

Hicks left and Burke sighed a breath of relief. He finished disconnecting the hard drives and pocketed them. He closed all the computers and unplugged them. They would have to take them all off the boat, and if Burke was the one to unload them, no one would ask about the missing drives. He stacked the computers and started putting them in their respective bags. As he bent over for Hudson's bag and stood back up, Hudson grabbed his arm. Burke almost had a heart attack until he realized Hudson's eyes were as lifeless as they had been. He brushed Hudson's hand off. He played it off as just a reflex, but what if Hudson did have enough sense to try and stop Burke? Would he be a problem?

Day 3

Upon Quint's decision to return to land, Hicks radioed ahead and let them know the situation. He reported they had one man overboard and missing, another dead, and one who was in a state of shock. As a result, the authorities were waiting for them when they returned. The coroner examined Lance and proclaimed him dead by broken neck by suicide. Rescue crews were dispatched to the area where they thought they lost Drake, and medical professionals gave Hudson an examination. He was alive, but unresponsive.

The Ontonagon PD had a lot of questions for the surviving crew. Each man was interrogated separately. Burke and Quint made no mention of losing consciousness. Quint because he thought he was awake all night and thought he might have nodded off at sometime before Drake went missing and Lance committed suicide. Burke merely stated that they were out on the lake all night and that he fell asleep in the cabin at one point. Hicks and Dorian did mention fainting, but neither of them mentioned what they saw or felt. The police were left scratching their heads by midday when the interrogations were finished. As they discussed what to do, Burke approached the others.

"I think it might be best to call off the investigation."

"No shit," replied Hicks. "I'm never going on Lake Superior again."

"I hate it…" said Dorian.

"I've been through hurricanes friendlier than this oversized puddle," added Quint. "But, what about my money?"

"Oh, right… Your money. Well, since we're cutting the investigation short, I'll be cutting your pay as well."

Quint looked like he wanted to argue, but if he wasn't going to work for Burke anymore, there didn't seem to be much point in pressing him for all of his pay.

They were approached by an officer.

"Gentlemen, I'm Officer Harrison Deckard. Listen, due to the odd circumstances of this situation, the Ontonagon Police would appreciate it if no one left town while we're investigating."

"How long will that take?" asked Quint. "A working man's got to make a living."

"Indeed. Hopefully, not too long. Maybe until the end of the week. Until then, please don't go anywhere."

Three of the four looked at each other and tried to come to terms with their new imprisonment. It wasn't too much of a problem, but could cause certain complexities. For one of them, it didn't matter.

"So be it," said Dorian. "The only place I want to go right now is to bed," he said, walking off toward his motel.

Dorian wasn't as tired as he was depressed, having lost the locket that contained Cordelia's ashes. He didn't understand how it had happened. She had told him it was a dream, and yet, the ashes disappeared from around his neck as if he himself threw them into the lake. Could he have? He stared at his hand for a minute wondering if it had betrayed him. But considering the high strangeness of the whole event, he didn't think that was too likely. Perhaps Cordelia's ghost actually threw them overboard.

Dorian returned to his motel room feeling half-dead. The depression and exhaustion combined into one unholy force that conspired to make a fool out of him. He didn't want to go to bed—he feared what he might see, as if a premonition from an alternate life warned him that he would only see dark things and nightmares. But as he stood before the bed, his eyes shut and he faded from the world of the waking.

It was impossible for Dorian to discern how long he slept, but the entirety of day passed without him. Night came, and with it came another vision of his past love.

Dorian found himself standing on the beach of Lake Superior. He turned and saw the port to one side and the bridge out of town on the other. If he looked down the street, he could almost see his motel. He turned toward the lake and saw the same blackened clouds roll in. As they did, far off in the distance, just above the horizon, Dorian saw what he thought was a red moon. It concentrated on him and gave him chills. He turned to walk away and suddenly saw Cordelia.

"Is it actually you?" he asked. "Are you really here? Again?"

"I am," she said.

"But, I'm not connected to the Serpent."

Cordelia looked down and frowned. She took a few steps past Dorian. "I'm afraid that that isn't the case. You've actually been connected to the Serpent for a while now."

"How?" he said, turning to her. "By what power?"

Cordelia looked down again. When she did look up at Dorian, she had tears in her eyes. "I'm sorry…"

"Why are you apologizing? You had nothing to do with this."

"I'm afraid I did. Though, it wasn't by my choice."

"I don't understand. Cordelia, please, just tell me what the hell is going on?"

"No! Too much has happened already. You must leave Ontonagon at once! This investigation has set things in motion that could end in all your deaths and the deaths of hundreds or thousands of others! Please, leave."

"I can't. I have to get you out. If you're suffering, please tell me what I can do for you."

"You can't do anything for me. I'm a prisoner until the end of the time."

Dorian fell to his knees. There was an abyss where his heart had been.

"Please! Many more will die if you don't go."

"I don't care about anyone else!" shouted Dorian. "I just want you! You're the only thing that matters in this world. The rest of it can go to Hell!"

Cordelia tensed up, her shoulders almost meeting her ears. She looked like she had heard the worst blasphemy ever uttered. "This is bigger than us, James! We can't be selfish about this! I don't want anyone else to suffer the way that I am. The way some of *us* are. Two of your expedition are here with me. They were manipulated to their deaths. They don't deserve this! And now, madness creeps within two others from your team. If you don't leave Ontonagon immediately, they'll be the next ones to join—!"

There was a bright flash of lightning and an ear-splitting crack of thunder. Cordelia turned toward the moon on the horizon and it somehow seemed pleased.

"It's too late…" continued Cordelia. "Another has joined us. Please, James; please, please, *please* leave Ontonagon. I don't want you to share the same fate as me."

Dorian was about to ask what fate that was when a warbling sound pierced his ear. The dream vanished and was replaced by a darkened room. Dorian didn't know where he was at first, but he could recognize the sound of a phone ringing. He grabbed the receiver from off the nightstand and brought it to his ear.

"Hello…?"

"Dorian! Dorian?! Is that you?!"

"Hicks? How'd you get this number? How'd you know which room I was in?"

"I asked the front desk. Listen to me, though, none of that matters. Something happened! Hudson is dead!"

Dorian paused. "…What?"

"Hudson is dead! His throat was cut in the night. I just got a call from the police. They're at the scene and investigating. They may be at your door any minute. I think they want to make sure we all have an alibi."

"Why? Who would kill…?"

"Dorian? Are you still there?"

"…Hicks. Have you called Burke yet?"

"I have. I couldn't reach him."

"You don't think—"

"That he killed Hudson?! Of course, I do! Lock your door and be careful. Burke may be coming after all of us. I don't know what happened to him out on that lake, but I think he lost it just as much as Hudson did. He wasn't acting right."

"Yeah…" Dorian felt shivers all over his body. Was this what Cordelia meant when she said "another" had joined them?

"Dorian. I'm going to call Quint. I'll call you in the morning."

"Sure thing," said Dorian as he hung up the phone. He then proceeded to make sure his door was locked and his shades were pulled.

What could have gotten into Burke?

Day 4

Dorian awoke the next morning, but didn't rise. He didn't see the point in doing so. There was nothing out in the world for him, and the police ordered that he stay in Ontonagon. He also wasn't sure he could depend on what Cordelia had told him in his dream. What could he have possibly done that would set off a chain reaction that would lead to all their deaths? What sort of power did the Serpent have and what was it doing to her and why? What did it want?

Dorian flipped onto his back and stared at the ceiling. He dozed with his mind focused on nothing, and soon deeper sleep found him. In the dream, he was transported to somewhere beneath the waves. He wasn't sure how he knew this, but he did. He could feel the chilly caress of smooth water all about his body as it supported him and he felt as if he couldn't breathe. He took a deep breath despite being under water and tried to hold it.

Just beneath him, Dorian could see what looked like Cordelia as she floated in the water. She had her eyes closed with her hands over her ears. She was screaming, but there was no sound coming out of her mouth. Dorian didn't know what could be tormenting her so until he saw it—in the sky above the lake and piercing through the water was the red moon. Its rays reached them, even in the depths, bathing them in its red light.

Dorian moved downward and tried to embrace Cordelia to protect her from the moon, but she passed right through his arms. Was it because she was a ghost, or because this was actually a dream? He couldn't tell, but he tried again and again to hold her or make some effort to comfort her, but he couldn't touch her nor could she hear him.

Dorian couldn't help but wonder what was causing her so much torment, and as if on cue, he felt what she felt—a sinister gaze that pierced right through his soul. The unrelenting pressure of the horror that something unnatural was staring at him and that there was nothing he could do to stop it. The feeling that there was no escape from that fear and that he'd be forced to experience it every hour of every day until the end of time was more than Dorian could bear. But the horror and dread wasn't all there was.

Dorian could feel every negative emotion he had ever experienced well up inside him. He felt hatred, anger, envy, pride, fear, and greed all surge within him. They reached an unspeakable height within his body, and Dorian could feel himself changing. He felt his features extend and his skin transform into plates. He became more accustomed to the water and he had the worst headache in his life as he felt his eyes burn. His eyesight turned red and he could feel his eyes begin to shift to either side of his head as his nose grew.

The negativity welled up inside him and expanded as he expanded. They filled every part of him and continued to push further out. Dorian tried to resist the change, but the power of his negative emotions was too strong. It wasn't long until his head hurt as he felt two protrusions extend from either side of his head. His arms and legs began to disappear and in their place formed a serpentine body.

Dorian looked up at the moon and began to curse it, when he realized something else. He looked around and noticed a knot of coils surrounding him and Cordelia. Dorian worried that it was the Serpent, but when he saw hundreds of eyes, he realized that the coils were actually hundreds of sea serpents. As they wriggled and snaked back and forth, Dorian could see them undergo similar transformations as he had. They drifted between human and serpent with most of them settling on the serpent form. Dorian stared in abject horror and he felt the water around him change for a grayish muck, just as he had seen in his first nightmare aboard the plane. There was also a penetrating stench of sulfur.

The muck turned back into water and Dorian looked back at Cordelia. He could see her body trying to make the same transformations manifest, but she would clench her fists and scrunch up her face and the transformations would subside. She was fighting the transformation, but more than that, Dorian realized she was fighting back the black emotions that harbored the change. She was fighting the fear, the hatred, and the anger. Occasionally, her face would return to a peaceful look.

Dorian wanted to reach out to her, to protect her from these maddening transformations, but he didn't know how to without being able to touch her. He screamed her name as loud as he could in his mind, hoping that whatever connection they shared would allow her to hear him. She seemed to as her eyes flicked open and she looked up at him. But the face that greeted Dorian was not one of affection, but sheer horror. He couldn't figure out why until he moved toward her, and instead of doing so with his hands and feet, he slithered through the water. The revelation of what he had become was enough to shock him out of his dream and back into the world of the waking.

He sat on his bed sweating and breathing hard. Had Cordelia actually seen him? Had she seen him in serpent form? But Dorian chided himself for thinking that because that wasn't what he should've taken away from that experience. What mattered was that that was the torture Cordelia had told him about—how she was suffering. Dorian had had no idea. The Serpent was actually trying to force her into contorting herself into a look-a-like by summoning all of her negative emotions and enhancing them. It was trying to turn her into a monster. And what was worse, there were other spirits of the dead there who accepted that fate, and may have even preferred it to being human. But what did that mean for the lake, the creature, and all the sightings? What was the goal? And what was the Serpent really?

Day 5

Dorian hadn't slept a wink since he dreamt about Cordelia's predicament. He couldn't close his eyes again. Every time he did, he saw those misshapen creatures, caught somewhere between monster and man. He saw Cordelia's struggle and pain, and worst of all, he saw the horror on her face when she saw him. He couldn't bear to see that face again. He had spent the rest of the night and the following morning thinking about how to rescue her, but nothing came to mind. He didn't know what sort of force was keeping her prisoner, and he didn't know if he could even understand what it was. He needed answers, but he didn't know what sort of questions to ask to get them or even whom to pose them. Frustrated with his lack of ideas, he went out for a walk in the late morning air.

Dorian wandered the town in a daze. The likelihood of him being able to save Cordelia seemed less and less with each passing second. He even tried considering the paranormal as this was a supernatural phenomenon. But, he was a man of science and therefore completely out of his element. Was there anyone in the whole world who could help him? Sure, many probably claimed to free souls, but had they ever taken on an entity like the Serpent before? What even was it?

Dorian came to the bridge out of town. He stopped midway across it and looked at the lake. Despite its impossible size, it seemed peaceful in the summer sun. Who would have thought such evil lurked beneath its waves?

It was at that moment that Dorian felt his skin crawl. He didn't know what caused it, but as he looked around, at one end of the bridge, he saw something that sent shivers through his body. He saw a man, but there was something wholly unnatural about him—he was staring right at Dorian with the deadest eyes possible as if the man was seeing his destiny, but it was a destiny Dorian didn't wish to share. He could feel the madness burning behind the man's eyes consuming him. The man headed toward Dorian with a shaky but quick walk and Dorian began to panic. He looked around for help, but the man had closed the distance with seemingly inhuman speed.

"Sanity rent by madness pure. Eyes of the dead conspire against the living. Macabre curiosity lures living to the dead."

Dorian shook to hear him speak. What sort of mad prophecy was this?

"A cursed death lends to a cursed afterlife. Life is but a dream and death a reality."

"By divine begot, by betrayal born, by vengeance unleashed. Ancient horror long forgotten called to the surface once more. Former enemy, now ally by will bequeathed."

"Shaman saw, sealed, and buried...

"False visions build belief beyond the seal, constructing reality in spite of reality, the seal is defied... Death reconciles with death—the Serpent is death—the Serpent is salvation."

Dorian jumped. He knew better than to trust the words of a mad man, but this might be the clue he needed that could lead him to freeing Cordelia. "The Serpent? Who are you? And what do you know of the Serpent?"

"Fear welcomes all, death accepts all fearful—to fear is to die—the Serpent is death. To live with memory is torture—to die to memory is solace, the Serpent is salvation."

"What? I don't understand. How could the Serpent be both death and salvation?"

"Seek not the Serpent, Contemplate not the Serpent, See not the Serpent, Record not the Serpent, Join the Serpent.

"Sanity is rent by curiosity misbegotten—seek not, contemplate not—soul rent by eldritch demon—see not, record not—Join... The Serpent is salvation."

That answer didn't make sense to Dorian. Regardless, he had other things to worry about. "How do I free those who are prisoners of the Serpent?"

"Devote not oneself to the dead; simply die. Sacrifice not for the dead; simply die. Pity not the dead; simply die. Love not the dead; simply die. Remember not the dead; simply die.

"Rue life, disdain memory—the dead belong with the dead—all life from water, to water all death. Ancient beast demands satiety—madness is the punishment for denying the demon its due—Life evokes it, death sustains it... The Serpent is death.

"Harbor not the dead among the living—linger with the dead as the dead. Go to the bulwark, and find salvation."

Dorian was beyond confused. He had never heard such nonsense. It sounded like this fellow wanted him to purposely die to the Serpent. But, why?

"Who are you?" asked Dorian, but the man wouldn't answer. Some of his personality had reappeared in his eyes and he didn't seem so scary. Despite this, he didn't respond.

"Who are you?!" repeated Dorian.

Dorian reached out to him when he heard someone shouting.

"Hey, you! What do you think you're doing?!"

Dorian looked over the man's shoulder and saw four men dressed in white charge down the bridge. They tackled the man and pinned him to the ground. He went without a fight. Another man in a brown suit accompanied by a police officer ran up.

"Well, well," said the man. "It's about time we caught up with you. Who knows what you might've done on your own. Take him back to the asylum," commanded the man.

The four men in white lifted the stranger to his feet and escorted him over to an awaiting vehicle marked "Ontonagon Rest Home".

The man in the suit turned to Dorian. "It looks like he was talking with you. What did he say?"

"I'm sorry, but—"

"Oh, right. Where are my manners? My name is Dr. Joseph Tyrell. I work at the Ontonagon Rest Home."

"I'm Dr. James Dorian. I'm a marine zoologist."

"Ah! Perhaps that's why Hendrid was called to you."

"I'm sorry?"

"That man is Hendrid Cold. Or at least he was. He lost his mind after he saw Lake Superior's monster apparently. Maybe he was drawn to you." Dr. Tyrell laughed.

Dorian didn't pay Dr. Tyrell any attention. He knew he had heard that name somewhere before. He snapped his fingers when he remembered. That was "Uncle Hendrid", uncle to the little girl he spoke to on his first day in town when he and Hicks were interviewing eyewitnesses.

"So, back to my question," started Dr. Tyrell, "did he say anything to you?"

"No," said Dorian. "He just stared at me."

"Are you sure? I thought I heard him say something. Didn't you ask him who he was?"

"Well, yeah, sure. Anyone would. A strange man approaches you and stares, wouldn't you ask him who he is?"

Dr. Tyrell's vision narrowed. "I suppose…"

"Come on, Doc," said the cop. "Let's get this nut back to the home. I have paperwork to fill out."

"Okay. Well, see you around, Dr. Dorian," said Dr. Tyrell as he allowed the police officer to drag him away.

Dorian watched as the four men loaded Uncle Hendrid into the back of the van. Before the doors shut, he locked eyes with Dorian who felt a chill run down his spine.

Uncle Hendrid's piece echoed through Dorian's mind and another tingle went down his spine. He was bothered by some of the things Uncle Hendrid had said. What did he mean by "By divine begot, by betrayal born, by vengeance unleashed. Ancient horror long forgotten called to the surface once more. Former enemy, now ally by will bequeathed"? And then there was "Shaman saw, sealed, and buried" and "False visions build belief beyond the seal, constructing reality in spite of reality, the seal is defied". What shaman? What seal? What belief? Dorian only had more questions now. He scratched at his head, frustrated.

"What does any of it mean?! Is it some sort of origin story?"

That's when Dorian had a brain wave. An origin story. That's what it was. It was the origin story of the Serpent. More specifically, it was the origin of the current phenomenon; after all, Uncle Hendrid only had this sort of insight after seeing the creature, so it must have been true. But if the Serpent had been sealed by a shaman, how did it escape again? Or did it? Is that what "False visions build belief beyond the seal, constructing reality in spite of reality, the seal is defied" meant?

Dorian scratched his head again. Why was it that some of what Uncle Hendrid had said made sense, but other parts didn't? Dorian pushed that question out of his mind and tried to concentrate on what had been said. He had a feeling that there was some wisdom in the man's madness and madness in his wisdom, but how did he separate one from the other? The part about the shaman stuck out to Dorian in a way the other parts didn't. There was something to it…

Dorian had another brain wave.

When they first set out on the lake, they went to the spot where Hicks had his sighting. And he had mentioned how right there on the shore was the dig site for the excavation he had been a part of—the same excavation that led to his sighting. There was an important clue in that dig site, and Dorian had to find it.

He looked to the west, to the Porcupine Mountains in the distance. It would take him a while to get there, but he couldn't go by car in case the police were tailing him to make sure he didn't leave town, which meant he had to go by foot. So, he set off and tried to look as inconspicuous as possible.

***

Hours had passed and night had fallen. Dorian was weary and drenched in sweat. He had followed along the I-64 as it traced the northern edge of the Upper Peninsula. When it ended, he passed through the small town of Silver City and along the next road called the 107th Engineers Memorial Highway. As he walked along it, he was already seeing signs for the Porcupine Mountains as well as their devastated terrain. He finally came to a toll entrance which was blocked by a chain link fence next to a sign that read Porcupine Mountains State Park.

Dorian collapsed on the ground and rested for a minute, trying to catch his breath and think of a way through the fence. Unfortunately, the only thing that floated through his mind was Uncle Hendrid's creed about the Serpent. It had occupied him since he left Ontonagon, echoing in the reaches of his mind. He felt he could understand some of it, but not all of it. Several clues were still missing, hence why he came to the Porkies. He needed to make it to the excavation site near the Presque Isle River.

Dorian recovered from his walk and looked at the fence again. There was a double gate chained closed and held by a padlock that kept the road into the Porkies secure. Dorian didn't know how he could get past that as someone had taken the liberty of lining the top of the fence with razor wire.

Dorian crept closer to the gate and noticed some give in the chain. He found that if he pulled both sides of the gate as far apart as possible, he could slip through them and under the chain. He waited for a lull in the traffic and forced his way through. It was still a tight squeeze, and one he almost didn't make, but as he wrenched himself through, his back foot just escaped the glancing blow of a car's headlight. He lay still on the ground and waited for the car to drive away. When it was gone, he bounded up and rushed into the park. He went back to the water's edge and continued west toward the Presque Isle River.

It was very late now—it must've been past midnight. Some clouds had rolled in, so there was no light coming from the sky. That made it dark, but to Dorian it seemed darker than normal. There seemed to be a black fog cast over the whole scene. Ashen and charcoaled trees stood all around him, their twisted branches forming a spider web of even darker shadows above him as if a net hung overhead. It was deathly quiet. He hadn't heard a noise since passing the visitor center. Not even the lake or the wind made a sound. The deathly stillness of it all unnerved him to the point where he thought he was going to scream. But as the fear crept into his throat, something caught his attention.

Dorian whipped around and faced the lake. He could see two piercing, red eyes light up beneath the surface. A shadowy body formed that was darker than the abyss of the lake. Dorian felt that this wasn't the Serpent, but one of its enslaved souls that had been recreated in its image. He could tell that it was similar to the creature he saw on the first day in the waves when he was investigating with Hicks. He had tried his best to keep the sighting from entering his mind, afraid that it would make him go crazy. But after everything he had seen so far, he feared he had little sanity left, and even then, it wasn't what he cherished most. A brown-eyed redhead entered his mind. Dorian focused on Cordelia's image, and he could feel the shadow serpent disappear. That was good news as Dorian could now focus and look for the site.

Dorian found the excavation site. He recognized it from the descending layers of levels from where the team had dug. He stepped down into the site and began sifting around. He wasn't entirely sure what he was looking for, but he thought he would recognize it if he saw something sticking out of the ground.

He continued to rifle around in the dirt, but couldn't find anything. Nothing seemed out of place, and apparently nature had started to take back the dig site. Fresh dirt and ashes were strewn about and some of the levels were misshapen. He stood up and glanced around, but in this sort of darkness, it was hopeless. He couldn't see anything.

"Aw, dammit!" Dorian cursed as he kicked one of the levels. "Damn, damn, damn! I was so close…"

"Close to what?" said a familiar voice.

Dorian straightened and turned. "Hicks? Is that you?"

"Yeah." Hicks walked out of the tree line, but all Dorian could see was his profile. "What're you doing here, Dorian?"

"I was…looking for a clue."

"A clue to what?"

"The Serpent. You said you saw it after you placed your hand on some relic. I thought if I could find it, it might offer some insight on what we're dealing with."

"Don't lie to me, Dorian," said Hicks. "Burke called off the expedition. *You* of all people should be relieved that it's over. Why are you actually here?"

"I told you: to find the relic."

"All right, that part I believe. But I don't believe the part about you looking for 'insight' into it. What insight could it offer? Three of our team are dead and another is missing. Going looking for relics is the last thing we should be doing."

Dorian thought about his plea. "Look, I've seen some things. Things you wouldn't believe."

"Oh, yeah? Try me."

"I've had more than one dream where I speak to my dead girlfriend who claims to be a prisoner of the Serpent. So I'm looking for the relic you found when you first had your sighting. I thought it might help me save her."

Hicks paused. "You're right… I don't believe you."

"I know it sounds crazy—"

"Oh, no. It's definitely crazy."

"—but if there's something I can do to save her, I have to try. Won't you help me look for it?"

"Dorian…you're messing with powers you can't understand. It killed one of us, possibly two of us, and it might be responsible for the madness of another and the murder of a fourth. It put us into a trance for an entire day and a good part of the night. If anything you say about your girlfriend is true, I doubt you alone can help her."

"Well, it's a good thing you showed up then. Come on, partner. Let's look for that relic."

"Dorian!"

"Please! What's it going to hurt to find it?"

"After everything we've been through, I think discretion is the better part of valor. Now, come on. Let's get out of here before something bad happens to us."

"Too late!" said a third voice.

"Burke?!" said Dorian.

"Oh, fuck," said Hicks.

"Hello, boys!" said Burke as he stepped from the tree line. The other two couldn't see him too well, but with how he was holding his arms out in front of himself, he looked like he was holding a gun. "Who knew the two of you were harboring such interesting secrets?!"

"It's not my secret," argued Hicks.

"Dorian! That's an interesting theory you have, hoping to save your dead chickie-poo with the power of a fetish. What do you intend to do? Hold the Serpent hostage until it releases her?!"

"I didn't really have a plan…"

"'Didn't have a plan', he says. I'm sure. Dorian, that's not the first lie you've told tonight. You tell me another and you're going to share the same fate as Hudson!"

Hicks advanced on him. "You son of a—!"

Burke swung the gun around and there was a click. Hicks stopped.

"Now, then, Dorian, tell me, what was your plan?! Does it have anything to do with what that mental patient whispered to you in Ontonagon?"

"How do you…?"

"I've been watching you, Dorian! Ever since I finished Hudson, you've been my prime target. You seem to be affected by the Serpent in a way that Quint and Hicks aren't. I heard you blubber on the boat. It might be true what you say about your dead girlfriend, and maybe that's why the Serpent targeted us. It was because of her! Because of her connection to you!"

Dorian felt a chill go down his spine.

"That's right, Dorian! She betrayed you! She might not have meant to, but that doesn't mean she didn't. Anyway, it's an interesting theory about you being able to set her free with the relic. I wonder what else it could be used for." Burke swung around. "Hicks, be a good man and find that relic, would you?"

"Burke, listen to me—"

A loud bang cracked the quiet night air and a brilliant flash of light briefly lit the scene.

"I've already heard it, Hicks! I'm not interested in your rationale. I have my own mission to accomplish. Now, find the damn relic, or die."

Hicks moved sideways as Burke kept the gun pointed at him. He stepped down into the excavation site and started poking around a pile of dirt on the far side. He began digging.

"Dorian! Help him move it along!" Burke commanded.

Dorian did so, and the two of them dug through the dirt like dogs. After a minute, they found a corner poking out of the ground. They continued digging down discovering what may have been a pyramid as there were three sides leading away from it. They continued digging, slowly revealing what turned out to be a black box. As they did so, the night became chillier and that existential dread they had both felt back on the boat began to permeate the air.

Hicks' digging speed slowed dramatically. He looked at Dorian. "I don't think we should do this," he whispered.

"It's too late now," Dorian whispered back. "Burke knows it's here. If we refuse, he'll kill us and just dig it up himself."

"No talking!" ordered Burke. "Keep digging!"

After a few minutes, Dorian and Hicks were forced to rip chunks of dirt out of the ground in order to free the box. With a few final tugs, they were able to pull it free. Hicks held it in his hands, stunned, before turning to Dorian. Dorian was equally confused.

"Well?!" said Burke.

"It's here," said Hicks, standing. "But…"

"But what?"

"This is odd. This box feels like it's made of plastic. Which, obviously, shouldn't be."

"Are you sure it's the right relic?" asked Dorian.

"Yeah. This is it all right. One foot by one foot, in that spot, and scares the hell out of me just holding it."

"And yet, there's nothing here," said Dorian.

"What do you mean?"

"You said that when you touched it, you had your sighting. There's nothing here."

"I can't explain that…"

"Let me see!" demanded Burke, excited.

Burke walked over to them and as he stepped down into the excavation site, Hicks and Dorian saw their opening. Hicks threw the box at Burke and Dorian dove for the gun. All three men fell to the ground and started throwing up dirt in their scuffle. Burke did his best to control the gun, but he also tried desperately to cling to the box. He tried to throw Dorian off the gun and bring the box closer. Doing so forced all three men to fall on top of each other, and each one of them placed a hand on the box. A shockwave of energy expanded outwardly from the box and threw all three of them onto their backs. Despite not being knocked unconscious, their visions began to darken.

The darkness was stripped away and there stood a man in the middle of a forest. He took out a lighter and lit it. He tossed it into the brush, the flame twirling. A mighty fire rose and enveloped the entire woodland. The man stood there watching the fire with nary a thought in his mind other than it was pretty to watch and its heat was just as intense.

The man turned. His head was held at an angle with a sardonic smile plastered on his face. His eyes were devoid of sanity. He looked at his guests; there were six in total. They were bound and gagged, standing atop barrels with a length of rope wrapped around each of their necks and then wrapped around a tree branch above. The man stepped up to the first victim and seemed to consider him. His eyes were focused on the man, but his mind had to be empty of all thought. The mad man's smile increased slightly and he accused the man on the barrel of this being all his fault. He placed a foot on the barrel and pushed it out from under the other, letting gravity and the rope do its work. There was a gargled response and a snapping sound as the rope pulled taut. The other five victims were incensed. They offered him curses that couldn't be made out due to the gags. The mad man then moved to the next one down the line and he lost his fury to madness.

Dorian watched the hideous scene unfold slowly and deliberately. Each victim had a fresh expression of horror and shock, and made their own death croak as they were systematically lynched. And as the maniac reached the last victim, Dorian made another horrifying discovery—all the victims were Native American. This wasn't just a mass murder, but a hate crime. The man was a racist, along with being an arsonist and psychotic.

The psycho reached the last victim, a woman. As he placed his foot on the barrel beneath her, she managed to chew her way through the gag and spit it out. She shouted at him in a language Dorian didn't understand, but it was clear that her words were pungent and carried a gravitas that no one would've wanted aimed at them. She continued to spit and hiss, but the mad man registered no emotion other than his blank smile. He accused her as he did the others that this was all her fault, and then he gave her a short drop and sudden stop. The girl didn't croak, but instead, there was a pained sigh from deep within her throat that contained a curse for the ages.

A black mist escaped her mouth and flew off toward the center of a massive lake as the maniac ran off into the burning forest. The black mist found the center of the super lake and travelled down to the abyss. It penetrated water, flora, and fauna until it reached the very bottom. There, Dorian's perspective passed down through the floor of the lake and into a different dimension altogether. There he saw a vast cavern that stretched beyond the limits of his vision. It was full of stalagmites and stalactites, and rock varieties he had never seen before. The cavern had no source of light, but Dorian could still see within it. But besides the cavern's features, there was only shadow and abyss here. He was more terrified than he had ever been before, but couldn't figure out why. That's when he saw the black mist permeate through the ceiling of the cavern and come to rest on a spot of the abyss. Two blank eyes opened, bathing the cavern in red light, and that's when Dorian saw it—the Serpent.

Its head rose and there was a primeval quake throughout the cavern as the entire creature's body moved. Dorian expected to see it slithering out of the darkness, but its body was the darkness. Coil after monstrous coil, the entirety of the cavern's oblivion was the totality of the Serpent's being. It passed through the ceiling of the cavern and in a winding motion, slithered its way through the great abyss of the lake itself. It broke through the bulwark that separated its resting place from the world of the living. Not only was the enchantment upon it finally broken, but the curse of one who once called it enemy summoned it to seek revenge.

The Serpent found the shore, but as it waded through the water, it saw the fire that razed the forest, the six victims, and the body of its quarry, charring within the flames. Its attempt at revenge had been foiled by the very madness of the one it was meant to hunt down. The Serpent, however, felt no disappointment. The man's soul would linger within the forest until the end of the world, and besides, the Serpent had won a much greater prize. The Serpent took the soul of the one who summoned it and the souls of those whose hatred had fuelled the spell. Those souls had offered themselves up in the name of revenge, and whether the Serpent was successful or not, it would take them regardless. Six dark souls, each looking like one of the victims, appeared in attendance of the Serpent before it melded into the water.

The scene changed and the fire went out. Only charred trees remained except for the lone tree and the six bodies that hung from it. An elderly Native American medicine man approached the grizzly scene and nearly collapsed with grief. He held his fist to his mouth as tears flowed down his face. His sobbing was erratic. His lament was so stricken that it caught the attention of a certain dark creature. It broke the surface of the bulwark from miles away and the medicine man gasped. He shot to his feet and looked out over the lake, his tears replaced by fear. He began to hyperventilate as he tried to remember the ritual that would seal the foul creature in the world beyond theirs, but it was no use—he couldn't remember it. Despite that, he did what he could and with a ritualistic chant and dance, he sealed the creature behind a veil that loosely separated the world of the living from the world of the dead, and to ensure that the creature would remain there, he made a figurine of it and placed it in a box. A physical representation of his spell would hold better than none at all. He then buried it within the ground near the site of the lynching for safekeeping.

The medicine man fully intended on returning and completing the spell, to seal the Serpent back within the depths of Hell, but on his way to learn it from a neighboring shaman, he was struck by a stroke and died. There the Serpent would sit, cut off from the living world for six years, but it did not spend its time idly. It turned to the six souls it collected and tortured them until they turned into weak facsimiles of itself, but far more terrifying than any of the fake serpents Dorian had seen so far. They ventured around the lake and killed any unsuspecting person they could and collected the soul, in turn transforming the newly acquired prisoner into one of them. Those new serpents would then travel the lake and build the story of the Serpent's existence in hopes someone could be tricked into releasing it upon the world. But the labor to set itself free was long and tedious.

The Serpent had amassed an army, but it hadn't come any closer to setting itself free. It transmitted a message out into the rest of the world for what could only be described as help. Dorian couldn't imagine who or what would respond, until a much darker and much larger presence appeared. Dorian had felt small compared to the Serpent, but compared to this leviathan, he felt tiny and inconsequential, as if comparing himself to the size of the solar system.

The LEVIATHAN responded transmitting images back of three individuals that it had seen through one of its facsimiles or from other monsters. These three were shown in blinding succession, but their visages were was unmistakable: Burke, Hicks, and Dorian. Burke was already being misled, the Serpent would have to get Hicks itself, but the LEVIATHAN would help with Dorian. Another image flashed of a beautiful girl diving in the Atlantic Ocean when an unseen being attacked her, and transported her soul to Lake Superior. Dorian felt a fury he never had before.

And so, with the conspiracy launched, the Serpent made sure that one of its prisoners promptly showed itself when Hicks discovered the box, and it was all but a matter of time from there. The Serpent even took possession of a living mind to make sure the three men would find their way to the relic and release it. And with that, the vision ended.

Dorian did his best to get a hold of himself. He was drowning in a cold sweat and couldn't stop hyperventilating. Although he was furious for being tricked into coming to Lake Superior, and he couldn't forgive Cordelia's death, when he had seen the truest nature of the Serpent, and the LEVIATHAN that seemed to be its master, he was shaken to his very core and questioned everything he thought he knew or believed in. What sort of power *was* he up against? And why was he foolish enough to think he could challenge it? Cordelia was right—there was nothing he could do for her.

He struggled to sit up, and as he did so, wondered why he couldn't see anything. He feared he had gone blind until he realized where he was. He looked around in a panic, looking for either the box or Burke, but both were gone. Dorian stood and looked in every direction; he had to stop him.

Dorian was about to take off when he heard groaning from the ground. He jumped, but realized it was Hicks.

"What the hell was that?!" said Hicks, sitting up. He looked up and saw Dorian. He jumped to and looked around.

"Burke is gone," explained Dorian.

"Damn! Did he take the box with him?"

"I think so."

"Why?! What the hell is he thinking? He saw the same vision as us. That box belongs in the ground. That shaman put it there for a reason. You don't think he intends on setting the Serpent free, do you?!"

Dorian shrugged. "I don't know."

"We need to find him. And fast!"

"We won't be able to find him tonight. There are too many places he could be. It'll be impossible to track him down in the dark."

"What do we do then?" asked Hicks.

"We could report him to the police for violating the dig site and for stealing artifacts."

"Won't that raise suspicions about how we know that?"

"We'll just tell them we tracked Burke here. They'll set up a search for him."

"Are you sure?"

"He's wanted in the questioning of Hudson's murder. They'll look for him."

Hicks stood. "Why do you think he didn't kill us? I mean, he woke up first."

"Maybe it was more important to him to escape with the box. He has his treasure. He just needs to enact his plan now. We're of less importance."

"If he does intend on setting the creature free, why didn't he just toss the box out into the lake here?"

"Maybe that's not his whole plan. Or maybe he wants to set the creature free out in the middle of the lake. You know, he wants to be symbolic about it."

Hicks grunted. "What the hell happened to him?"

Hicks and Dorian hobbled their way out of the park and a made call to the police with the nearest phone they could find. The police arrived as soon as they could, which given their location, was not quick. The police took their statement and asked them several questions, such as why did they break into the park after they saw Burke enter it. They made up the story that they thought they knew what he was after and thought they could stop him. The officer told them they were dumb for doing so.

The officer finished with his questions and told them they'd start a trail on Burke tomorrow. He then offered to give them a ride back to Ontonagon.

It was the first time Dorian had ever been in the back of a police car. It was another novel experience that he got to have on this expedition.

He leaned his head against the window and closed his eyes. Sleep found him quickly, and almost as quickly, so did Cordelia. She appeared on the seat next to him, between him and Hicks. She didn't look happy to see him.

"I told you to leave! I told you and told you and told you. I *begged* you to leave, but you wouldn't listen! And now, because of you the Serpent is closer than ever to being released. Thousands will die and Lake Superior will be overrun with the ghosts of the dead!" Cordelia started to pout. "Please! It's too late! You must leave. Leave Michigan behind and never come back!"

"After all I've seen? How can you expect me to leave now? You're right. This is my fault, and I have to clean it up. I *will* clean it up. Just need to find Burke. He's not on the lake, is he?"

"I don't know. I don't think so. I'm not connected to him. I'm connected to you… But…everything feels as it did. Nothing's more restless than it was. If he was on the lake, I expect I would feel something, but I don't."

"Then there's time."

"How do you intend to stop him?"

"Just need to get the box back. It contains the figurine of the Serpent, right? Just need to make sure that thing doesn't touch the water."

"You'll fail."

Dorian whipped around to look at her. "You've never doubted me before…"

"This is different. Your phobia was all in your mind. It was you versus yourself—how could you not win? But this…you're against a demon here."

Dorian chuckled humorlessly. "Ain't that a bitch? Looks like God is real after all. And he's got a twisted sense of humor, allowing something like that to exist."

"Please, James," she entreated, "just leave Ontonagon. Your quest to set me free has become too personal. The Serpent knows that all three of you are here. It knows that you're going to try to stop Burke. It will do what it can to stop you and make sure Burke succeeds. Please, just leave."

"No. This is my mess, and I'm going to clean it up."

Cordelia looked down into her lap. She grabbed Dorian's hand and squeezed it. "Good luck, my love. I'll see what I can do on my end. But once you stop Burke and get the box back, put it back in the ground. It can't set me free. Only the Serpent is connected to it, not me. I love you."

Dorian opened his eyes and felt Cordelia's grasp dissipate. He steeled himself for the task ahead.

Day 6

After being dropped off by the officer, Hicks and Dorian parted for the night. They had debated looking for Burke, but they were both exhausted by the night's activities and figured exhaustion would catch up with Burke in due time. Besides, they wanted to include Quint in their plan, and chances were good that he wasn't awake. So they waited for morning, but due to the nightmare vision they had both had, sleep didn't come easy, and what rest there was, was not restful. Nasty visions of serpentine demons, burning forests, hanging bodies, and murderous madmen haunted them. When the sun rose, they were both glad for it and wasted no time in departing.

Thinking the same thoughts, Hicks and Dorian showed up at the docks at the same time. And even greater fortune was with them when they saw Quint sitting on the deck of the Ripley, enjoying a cup of coffee.

"Good morning, lads," he said. "I wasn't expecting to see you today."

Quint looked at their somber faces, realizing this wasn't a casual meeting. "What happened?"

"We need to talk," said Hicks.

Quint invited them aboard and they went into the cabin. Hicks and Dorian recounted the previous night's events, including their ghastly vision. Quint went from concerned to terrified to alarmed as the conversation went on.

When they were finished, Quint stared at them for a second. "So, this *thing* is real?!"

"It gave us all nightmares only a few days ago, didn't it?" replied Hicks.

"It is real, but not as we understand it," said Dorian. "Somehow the shaman managed to seal it on the 'other side', whatever that is."

"And you reckon you know what Burke's plan is?"

"We think he intends to release it," said Dorian. "We can't say why, though."

"He's lost his damned mind," added Hicks.

Quint paused. "So, what's your plan then?"

"We need to stop Burke."

"No shit. But, how? Suppose he just tosses the figurine into the lake from the shore. Do you know how much of the Upper Peninsula touches Lake Superior?"

"I don't think he'll do that," said Dorian. "Burke seems to have a taste for the dramatic. He is a cryptozoologist after all. He's not likely to go about this in some half-assed way."

"Dorian thinks he's going to drop the figurine into the center of the lake."

"The *very* center?!" replied Quint. "That's about seventy nautical miles from here. Depending on the boat he intends on using, that could take him either all day to reach or he could be there in four to five hours. And there's no telling where he plans to leave from. Ontonagon isn't the only port in the Upper Peninsula."

"We get the picture, Quint," said Hicks annoyed. "It seems impossible, but we have to try. There's no telling what will happen when he releases that thing."

"Did you tell the Coast Guard?"

"We reported him to the police," replied Dorian. "They were supposed to start a trail on him from his last known location this morning."

"But the more people on his tail, the better," said Hicks. "We can call the Coast Guard if we spot him, but are too far to intercept."

"*If* we spot him," said Quint. "And that's a pretty big 'if'. Seriously, why don't we just skip town if this thing is that dangerous?"

"Because I'm responsible for this," answered Dorian.

"Say again?"

"I'm responsible for this. I went digging for answers where I shouldn't have, and now if this creature does get out of its imprisonment, I'm to blame. But I can't stop Burke on my own. I need a boat and lots of help. Please, Quint."

Quint fidgeted. "You two are operating on a lot of assumptions about Burke's character."

"We know," said Hicks.

"But given Burke's behavior, we think his next few actions are what we assume."

"Why?"

"Because they're exactly what I would do if I intended on setting the Serpent free." They're also how I would go about trying to set Cordelia free, Dorian thought. "You wouldn't get it, Quint. You didn't see the vision. Certain things just make sense."

Quint looked down at the table and sighed. "So, the plan is to patrol the shore from Ontonagon to the excavation site and hope for some luck? Is that about it?"

"Yes," said Dorian.

"I also wouldn't be surprised if when Burke does get on the water, we'll know by some sort of telepathic link," said Hicks. "Or, by the sky turning black again or something."

"Yeah. We can't miss him."

Quint exhaled through his nose. "So be it."

They wasted no time in getting to work. Quint had them shove off immediately and they started patrolling the shore from Ontonagon to the Porkies. As they passed by the park, they saw that the police were keeping their word by searching for Burke.

"Do you think we'll spot him?" asked Hicks.

"I don't know," said Dorian.

"Do you think we'll stop him?"

"I really don't know."

"I have a feeling deep down that we won't. I just can't shake it. I feel like Quint is right—we should just skip town. With each passing second, I feel like I'm getting crazier and crazier."

Dorian stared at Hicks with mild concern.

"How can you remain so calm, Dorian?"

"We have a task to complete. Just focus on that. Like you said, there's a good chance we'll know Burke's on the lake even if we don't see him. The ritual to release the Serpent likely won't be subtle."

"I feel like it's already here… And that I'm as good as dead."

Dorian didn't know what he could do for Hicks. He also had a deep seated dread about their task, but it felt somewhat muted. He didn't understand it himself. Perhaps he had just come to terms with the fact that he was probably going to die today.

They took the search in turns. One would drive while another scoured the shoreline while the third rested. They changed every hour, and for hours on end it seemed like nothing was going to happen, but both Hicks and Dorian knew that wasn't true. Something was going to happen today.

***

When Dorian wasn't on lookout, he rested in the cabin. He tried to sleep, but rest was never easy, and the only dreams he did have were of Cordelia pleading with him to leave. Even when he was awake, he swore he could just see and hear her. But he had to ignore her. He had a job to do. He kept repeating that to himself over and over, but it did little to bolster his confidence.

Eventually, he could feel himself just on the verge of sleep when he felt a long, taut sensation pulling at his gut. He had never felt anything like it before, but figured it was a muscle cramping. He tried to lie back, but the feeling increased in strength and that's when Dorian noticed that it was pulling him toward the center of the lake. His eyes widened as he felt a second string pull at him from Ontonagon and he had a clear vision of Burke piloting a boat on the lake.

Dorian jumped and ran out of the cabin. He shouted at Hicks and Quint, "I can feel him! I can feel Burke! He's on a boat back at Ontonagon, heading for the center of the lake!"

"Are you sure?!"

"Yes!"

Quint spun the Ripley around and threw it into full throttle. He plotted a course that would allow them to run into Burke as he headed for the center. And it wasn't long until Quint didn't have to take Dorian's word for it. The sky erupted into black cloud cover and looked like they had stumbled across the apocalypse as they had a few days previous. Quint reported their position and bearing to the Coast Guard, and reported Burke's destination, hoping they might be able to stop him before they got to him.

"Roger, Ripley!" the Coast Guard replied. "We have Burke's coordinates. Ontonagon PD report that you are not to go near Burke. Repeat, the Ontonagon Police don't want you going anywhere near Burke! Over."

"Are we going to listen to that?" asked Hicks.

"Of course not!" said Quint. "It'll take them too long to actually reach him." Quint turned a little more toward the center of the lake and made their approach steeper. They hit each wave with great impact as the boat pushed to reach twenty knots. The Ripley fought its way through the waves before giving away to another and sometimes flew off waves like a car flying off jumps.

"Quint! Take it easy," warned Hicks. "You go too hard and she'll start breaking up."

"No fears there," replied Quint. "We're catching up!"

Dorian and Hicks started at that answer, but as they looked at the lake, they could just see the remnants of a boat wake on the surface which they followed up to a white dot on the horizon that was getting bigger.

"It's time to pay the ferryman, Burke," said Quint.

Neither Dorian nor Hicks knew what he meant. They didn't have time to ruminate on it though as a bright flash of lightning illuminated the sky. It was close and looked as if it struck the lake. The boom of the following thunder almost deafened them. Dorian and Hicks looked at each other clearly worried as more lightning strikes hit the surface and thunder roared. The lake responded and the water became even choppier. They had been gaining on Burke, but now it looked as if they were losing him. The lake seemed to be calm for him and working against them. But they didn't have to guess at this as a giant wave began to form from their starboard side. It rose in size quickly, sucking water out from under the Ripley to add to its mass as it began to curve up and over.

"Brace for impact!" screamed Quint.

Dorian and Hicks jumped back down to the deck and wrapped their arms in remnants of rope, and hugged the deck floor with all their might as tons of water came crashing down. The Ripley rocked dangerously to one side, and every man aboard thought she was going to roll. Dorian was nearly thrown over the gunwale, and was only saved because Hicks had pinned Dorian against it. Quint had somehow held onto the wheel and was too stubborn to let go. But as all three of them looked into the depths of Lake Superior, a flash of lightning illuminated several long and massive bodies swimming to the surface. If they weren't chilled from the wave that hit them, their blood surely went cold from the sight of the Serpent's slaves. They rose and broke the surface. Each one was horribly grotesque in its own way and tested the limits of each man's sanity. One with a mouth big enough to swallow a man whole snapped at Dorian, but Hicks managed to pull him back to safety as the Ripley rocked back to starboard.

"Just like the vision…" said Hicks as he turned. In every direction he looked, he saw the surface of the Superior come alive with serpentine bodies. "They're all the dead souls *it* managed to capture…"

"Not all the dead souls. Lance, Hudson, and Drake are not among them." And neither was Cordelia. He knew that for a fact.

One of the lake monsters swam up alongside the Ripley and tackled her from the port side, rocking her violently. Another swam up from starboard and did the same. And then there was a sensation from below the bow as one hit them from beneath.

"God Almighty!" cursed Quint. "They're everywhere!"

"Keep going, Quint!" shouted Dorian. "Focus on Burke! You must. Don't look at them!"

Quint could feel his resolve slipping as the surface of the lake slithered with monsters, surrounding them on every side. He could feel that steel cage that kept his mind intact—the one that had allowed him to see so many strange and perverse things throughout his life without losing himself—begin to bend and break away. For the first time in his life, he refused to believe what he was seeing, and he knew that if he refused too hard, his mind would snap and that would be the end of him. He tried to maintain that delicate balance of sane and insane like a tightrope walker, and pulled his vision up to focus on Burke who was steadily getting away.

"What do we do?!" asked Hicks as another row of spines betrayed another impact from the right. "We can't keep this up. The boat will be torn apart and we'll be at the mercy of the lake!"

Dorian screwed up his eyes, and summoned Cordelia to him. He asked her for help. He then called up Lance, Drake, and Hudson, and did the same. Suddenly, the lake evened out allowing them to regain speed, and as the

Serpent's enthralled moved to strike the Ripley, they found themselves diverted by currents that hadn't been there a second ago. There were still good souls among the dead. But Dorian's relief was shattered as he, Quint, and Hicks had a sinking feeling.

Somewhere from deep within, they all felt as if something was sucking them toward the bottom of the lake and the world was rising above them, but it wasn't just the world—there was an ominous presence rising above them. It was the same presence they had felt on the night of the nightmare. The presence of the Serpent was climbing above their heads, and each man had the sensation that they were falling to the center of a funnel, and on all sides were the Serpent's enthralled as they swam around the maelstrom.

"Snap out of it!" demanded a voice.

Dorian blinked and shook his head. He looked around and found everything as it should have been. He could still feel the oppressive aura of the Serpent, but there was no funnel or maelstrom. Hicks and Quint didn't seem to know that though.

"Hey!" said Dorian as he slapped Hicks.

Hicks stumbled and knocked his head on the cabin wall. He shook his head and looked around, realizing it was just an illusion.

"Quint!" called Dorian. He started to climb up to the bridge, but as he got higher, he saw something that chilled him to the bone.

Rising from the depths of the lake were six shadows. They were serpentine like the rest, but they were much bigger. They burst out of the water and held themselves up as they matched the speed of the boat. These serpents towered over the Ripley by several stories. Their flesh was mostly rotten with parts of their skeleton exposed, giving off a suffocating aroma that nearly choked all three men. As Dorian tried to choke back the tears invoked by the stench, he instantly knew that these six were the original six that had been lynched those six years ago. Their hatred for the living, their proximity to the Serpent, and their desire for revenge allowed them to turn into the most horrifying of all monsters.

Dorian tried to cover his mouth and nose and continue climbing, but every fresh breath he took made him gag. He tried not to, but he couldn't prevent himself from vomiting as it seemed to be pulled up from the depths of his gut. He vomited down one side of the ladder, and as he did so, Hicks was also busy being sick down in the deck.

Dorian held onto the ladder and did his best to continue climbing, but every breath made him sicker and sicker. He couldn't stop retching, which threw him into a full-body heave. He gasped to get his breath back, but that only caused him to vomit more. His grip on the ladder began to weaken and he feared he would fall into a puddle of his own sick.

Dorian felt something move overhead and he looked up. He saw one of the serpents looming above them. It was the most grotesque of them all and the most foul smelling. Dorian held his breath as he looked up at it, sure he would soon faint from all the trauma he had suffered.

The serpent stared intently at Quint and Quint stared back, dumbfounded. It briefly glanced at Dorian with one dead eye and a vision shot through his head. He knew that this was the spirit of the single woman. It turned its attention back to Quint, and as all of its malice focused on him, the steel cage holding Quint's mind together buckled and shattered. He dropped to his knees and started laughing. It was such an uproarious and raucous laughter that it could be heard over the sounds of the crashing waves and echoing thunder. Quint didn't know who or what he was anymore, but he didn't care. He opened his arms wide and accepted whatever fate the woman had in store for him. The monster surged forward, and Dorian let go as fast as he could, falling down to the deck of the Ripley as the flying bridge became an explosion of splintered wood, shattered plexiglass, broken glass, and torn metal. Dorian came closer than he ever wanted to that serpent as it passed overhead, forcing the Ripley down into water as the creature disappeared into the lake, leaving a sizable wave in its wake that threatened to wash away both Hicks and Dorian. It took them a few seconds to recover, but when they did, the extent of the damage was clear, and they both felt pits in their stomachs deeper than they had ever felt before.

The entire bridge of the Ripley had been destroyed. Where the helm had once been was now empty air, and the bridge had been cut down to the roof of the cabin. Hicks and Dorian looked at each other, and both wondered what that meant for navigation. They looked over the cabin roof and noticed that Burke had stopped his boat. And as he was lifting the box up to the Serpent, Dorian and Hicks realized they were on a collision course.

Thinking as fast as he could, Hicks grabbed Dorian. "C'mon! To the bow of the boat!"

The two men fought their way over the wreckage and passed the cockpit to the bow pulpit. Each man placed a foot on the handrail and prepared for impact. Burke turned his head at the last second, just before the Ripley collided with him, throwing Hicks and Dorian over the rail and into the cockpit of Burke's boat.

There was a crunch and a creek as the Ripley slammed into the other boat. It threatened to remove the stern and outboard engine, but it didn't. It merely upset the boat's angle and rocked it violently. All three men were thrown to the boat's deck and rolled around. The Ripley continued on its course and headed for open water. In the other boat though, the three men struggled to get to their feet, each one disoriented. But as Hicks and Dorian assisted each other up, they came to the same realization and ran at Burke who stood near the bow.

Burke held the box over the guardrail, stopping Hicks and Dorian.

"Don't do it, Burke!" shouted Hicks.

"You'll kill us all!" added Dorian.

Burke remained silent for a minute, before saying, "You think it's easy, don't you? You think it's easy being a cryptozoologist. Travelling to far flung lands and the remotest parts of the world, looking for the undiscovered. Putting your reputation on the line and investing what little money you have into something that most likely won't turn a profit, but you do it anyway because you *believe*.

"You think putting this expedition together was easy?! Or cheap?! It wasn't!"

"Who cares about the goddamned money?!" shouted Hicks. "Or the fact that your life has been hard?! Four men are dead. Four! Because of this damn expedition. And look where we are?! We're on the threshold of Hell! We stand in the middle of an ancient lake, the portal to another dimension, surrounded by fucking ghosts and monsters, and you're threatening to release the king of them all! *We* likely won't survive this, but can you imagine how much more will be lost if you set that thing free?!"

"How much will be lost? How much have I lost?! What about me?! What about all the friends and credit I've lost?! Where's my recompense?"

"Who gives a shit about you?!" said Dorian. "This isn't about us—this is about the well-being of everyone! This is bigger than we could possibly imagine. It's a conspiracy against the whole human race!"

"Then think how I will be rewarded for my part in their liberation."

"What?!"

"What do you mean?" asked Hicks.

"Did you not hear it? At the end of the vision back in the Porkies, there was a voice that echoed. It said, 'Free me, and I will grant you a boon. Anything you desire will be yours.'"

"Anything?" repeated Dorian. He tried to sound dubious, but there was a tinge of hope in his voice.

"You're crazy, Burke!" said Hicks. "You've got another thing coming if you think that thing will actually give you what you want. It's a fucking monster!"

"Well, I guess there's only one way to find out. After all, it's as you said—we are on the threshold of Hell. Other than my life, what else do I have to lose?"

"How about your *soul*, dumbass?!"

But Burke did not listen. Instead, he opened the box and pulled out a black, coiled figurine. Dorian and Hicks ran at him, but all Burke had to do was let go, and he did.

Hicks tackled Burke to the ground, yelling at him, "What have you done?!"

Dorian saw the figurine splash into the lake, and as he looked up, he swore he could see Cordelia's dejected face. "I'm sorry…"

As the figurine hit the water, the whole world seemed to shake and the water rippled before it began to bubble and boil. The boat shook and began to spin as lightning crashed down all around them and the lesser serpents shrieked. One lightning bolt struck the site where the figurine had fallen and all three men were deafened by the thunder that followed. They fell to the deck and shook. But then nothing happened. Everything was silent, the black clouds were gone, and the lesser serpents had disappeared. The three men stood up and looked around, bewildered. The only noise they heard was coming from the Ripley, still trolling off in the distance. The three men looked at each other.

"No!" shouted Burke. "No! No! No! It wasn't supposed to happen like this! It was supposed to be my defining moment! This was the proof I needed!"

Burke yelled up into the sky, but suddenly stopped. Hicks and Dorian looked at him and saw his eyes glaze over as he stared at the moon. They looked too and saw the moon turn blood red, casting a red pall over the entire lake. And as they watched the water turn red, a shiny black creature appeared before them.

Did it emerge from the depths of the lake, from the depths of their minds, or from the depths of Hell?

Its size was immeasurable, stretching from a point beyond their understanding, and coiling in on itself. Its form was twisted as if its skeleton had decided to contort but the body hadn't followed. Dorian couldn't tell if its ribs spread vertically like an eel's, or horizontally like a snake's. It was covered in scales so black they absorbed all light, making it so that they didn't so much see the Serpent, as much as they saw everything that wasn't the Serpent. But there were bits of it bathed in the light of the blood red moon, which revealed a latticing degeneration throughout its body. The blood red light revealed holes where its twisted skeleton and gelatinous organs could be seen, inducing nausea within them all.

Its head, however, was ugly beyond imaging and invoked the worst sort of dread. It was a serpent's head, but it was covered in hundreds of slavering mouths with a thousand red eyes, each one a pool of hatred and every villainy imaginable. Dorian had a flashback to his nightmare.

The Serpent's main mouth was where it was supposed to be, but it stretched nearly to the very back of its head. Its two largest eyes had no pupils and glowed such a red that the fires of Hell could have been birthed by the light they cast. And then there were its horns—these were no elk or goat's horns, but the horns of pandemonium. They were constructed from bones and lashed together by some dark fiber that held them rigid.

Its locomotion was incomprehensible as it possessed the ability to swim through the air like it was water, and fly through the water as if it was air. Such was its mass and movement that Dorian had the horrible feeling that its roiling created the very foundations upon which Hell now sat, and he had another flashback to his nightmare where he saw the swamp made of the souls of the dead through which a black coil would occasionally appear. He had another horrible feeling that what he saw here was merely a tiny part of something so large, it could have swallowed the galaxy—so how big was the LEVIATHAN?!

The Serpent's mind, presence, and bearing wholly consumed them and laid them bare. They held no secrets from the Serpent, but their existence seemed so inconsequential compared to it, no secret they could ever have would interest the beast. What were they to one of the greatest eldritch horrors in all of creation?

Burke cracked a smile and began to laugh. A horrible, humorless laugh. Dorian and Hicks looked at him with their eyes wide.

"It's beautiful!" declared Burke. "Oh! What a sight! My first true and only love! In its presence I swear my life and my death, and I renounce the dragon of light. Take me!"

Dorian and Hicks were so bewildered by Burke's vow that neither man was thinking when they saw him throw himself overboard and into the lake. They clenched their fists and waited, and after a pause, they weren't sure how they knew, but they knew Burke was dead, despite the fact the Serpent hadn't moved.

Dorian and Hicks looked at each other, and all at once, felt their attention demanded toward the Serpent. From where they stood on the boat's deck, they were level with the Serpent's eye, washing them with red light, and they felt its oppressive, hideous, and eldritch consciousness pierce their minds.

"And so," a voice whispered in their heads, giving them both a headache, "what reward do you wish for freeing me?"

Both men stood there, rooted to their spots. They were drenched in sweat, but their mouths had gone dry.

"What do you wish?!" said the voice again, rising and pushing them for an answer, but they still did not speak.

"Answer me!" said a booming voice. "Answer me! Or perish…"

Hicks whimpered, and a pulse of light was emitted from the Serpent's eye, throwing him overboard. He went in complete silence except for the splash he made, and somewhere in the depths below, Dorian knew he had met his end. In fact, his death was confirmed as another slavering mouth and another pair of red eyes opened on the Serpent's head, and Dorian saw that its horns grew an almost imperceptible amount. Its victims became a part of its mass.

Dorian stared into the Serpent's great eye and thought briefly about making a plea for Cordelia. He tried to sweep away the thought as soon as it appeared, not wishing to draw attention to her, but the Serpent was already inside his mind. No thought he had was his own anymore, and he couldn't do anything to keep the Serpent out. It would reside in his mind for as long as it pleased.

Dorian sweat under the scrutiny of the Serpent. It seemed to consider his fate more thoroughly. He could feel it probing his mind, swimming through it with the entirety of its great bulk. It gave him such a mind-bending headache, that he thought his skull was going to split. He begged for some sort of release—any kind of release. But the Serpent was considering him. For a demon of its age and power, very rarely did any human draw its curiosity. It was above the desires and thoughts of humanity, and instead was only invested in transcendental callings, such as pain and fear.

Dorian tried to think of Cordelia as a means to calm himself down, but he realized that was a mistake as he felt the Serpent have a revelation.

"Ah…" said the voice. "You! I know you…"

That was the last thing Dorian wanted.

"And I see what it is that you want. Releasing a soul imprisoned under me is within my power, but there is a complication…

"The soul you want is not imprisoned under me, but under my master, the LEVIATHAN!"

What little sweat Dorian had left in his body drenched his face. He didn't understand how what the Serpent said was possible, but he immediately understood the implications of trying to free her from it.

"For you see," continued the Serpent, "you've been a piece in our game for a very long time."

Dorian felt a rush as several images flew through his head. He was forced to travel backward through his memory till he stopped at a scene he knew well. He was back in Chile as a group of grad students busied themselves with brushing away the sand and dust from a fossilized skeleton in the ground. The head was revealed, and Dorian shivered in the past as he did now in the present—the head of this creature was the same as the head of the Serpent's. Dorian then felt his perspective change and he was now looking through the creature's empty eye sockets, staring at himself, and being evaluated. He felt as if he was a part of a much greater whole, and he was terrified for its mass and evil were beyond his comprehension. It knew everything about him in a single second and a plan was hatched in the next. Then in the third, Dorian saw a redheaded woman swimming under the water and being struck by an invisible force. He then saw as her likeness was communicated between the free LEVIATHAN and the trapped Serpent to be used as a means of luring Dorian to Lake Superior.

Dorian fell to his hands and knees with tears streaking down his face. Everything that had happened had been his fault—it had all been his fault from a time so long ago that he couldn't have even imagined it.

He lifted his head to the Serpent, utterly broken and mad. "Do it! Kill me!" he demanded. "I can't stand it anymore! Release me from this torture!"

The Serpent seemed delighted with this development, but it merely inhaled through its nostrils. It coiled back to the front of the boat and raised itself out of the water. Dorian saw the underside of the Serpent, which was composed entirely of the wailing souls of all its prey. He recognized some of the unfortunate souls among them—they reached out for Dorian, begging to be freed.

The Serpent rose more than fifty feet in the air and locked eyes with Dorian. A voice whispered through his mind, threatening to exorcise what little sanity he had left, "Your pain is my pleasure and your death my treasure. But…we have plans for you."

Dorian felt a new sense of horror and shock. What more could they want from him?!

New chills enveloped Dorian as he considered the possibilities, not even seeing the Serpent's mouth open, containing thousands of fangs. The Serpent struck with blinding speed and enveloped him in darkness, as a new voice echoed that shattered the remnants of Dorian's sanity.

Epilogue

Dorian jolted awake. He was in a white room, lying in bed. He knew where he was, but couldn't believe it—he couldn't believe he wasn't dead.

He attempted to sit up and reach for the call button, but every inch of his body hurt. He didn't remember receiving any injuries, but considering what he was last facing down, he preferred being alive and in pain to what he thought was going to happen.

A passing nurse saw him moving. "Oh! Dr. Dorian, you're awake. I'll fetch Dr. Silberman immediately."

Dorian exhaled. Hopefully, someone could fill him in on what happened.

The nurse returned promptly, but besides the doctor, there was also a man in a trench coat. Dorian thought he looked like a detective.

"Hi, Dr. Dorian. I'm Dr. Silberman. How are you feeling?"

"Everything hurts."

"Really? Interesting. You didn't have any wounds as far as I could tell. And you weren't injured at any other time…?" Dr. Silberman looked over at the detective who shook his head.

"Yeah, I can't explain it, either," said Dorian.

"I was hoping you could," said the detective.

"Dr. Dorian," began Silberman, "this is Lieutenant Traxler with the Ontonagon police. He has a few things he wants to ask you."

"I'm sure you have a number of questions, such as how you got here," said the Lieutenant. "And I can answer that for you if you're willing to answer a few things for me. I mean, if you're up to it."

"I'll answer what I can."

"Good. Well, you see, the Coast Guard picked you up while you were lying unconscious on a boat that had sustained some damage to its stern. They found the remnants of a boat called the Ripley not too far off. Also, we were under the impression that you were tracking a Paul Burke, and that you were in the company of a Michael Hicks. And the call to the Coast Guard was made from the Ripley, which was owned by Robert Quint. Can you tell us where any of those men are now and how things ended up the way they did?"

"I'm sorry," said Dorian. "I'm afraid I can't tell you anything other than that they are all dead."

Traxler recoiled. "What? What do you mean they're dead?"

"Like I said, I can't tell you anything."

"Why not?"

"You wouldn't believe me if I told you."

"I'm willing to give it a try."

"Really?!" said Dorian. "Tell me: what do you know of the Superior Serpent or of a creature known in Ojibwe myth known as the misiginebig?"

"I don't believe in monsters, Dr. Dorian."

"Then never mind what happened out there. Three men are dead. If you're not willing to go on a little faith, then there's nothing for you here."

Traxler's eyes narrowed. "I'll drop by tomorrow."

Dorian rolled his eyes as the lieutenant left. He looked at Dr. Silberman who also seemed a little put out. "Well, Doctor, when can I get out of here?"

"We'd like to keep you for a couple days at the least, especially since you said you're in pain, despite no obvious origins. We'd like to examine you. We'll give you a little something for the pain."

"Very well."

The doctor and nurse examined Dorian, but nothing was missing, and there wasn't a single scratch or bruise on him. However, he rated his pain at about a five out of ten, so they gave him some vicodin and wished him a good night's rest.

Dorian sighed and closed his eyes. When he opened them again, Cordelia was there sitting on his bed, giving him a pitying look.

"*It* is using you against me."

Cordelia looked away.

"But, so long as it has plans for me, I have plans for it. And for *all* of you," said Dorian as the ghosts of Hicks, Drake, Hudson, Lance, and Quint appeared.

Dorian closed his eyes again and focused on the last thing he had heard when the Serpent attacked him. "Seek not the Serpent—Seek the LEVIATHAN."

Becoming The Dragon

The Reading

It was a dark evening. The thunderstorm had rolled in much earlier than predicted. Despite the fact it was only 8:30 in July, it already looked like night due to the storm. But Elliot wasn't going to let a little rain dampen his evening. The day would be what he made of it.

He drove southbound on Gratiot Avenue heading to Roseville, a little suburb on the northeast side of Detroit. He was going to Madam Mystique's Fantastical Emporium. Elliot had passed by Madam Mystique's many times on his drive to and from work. The little shop had always fascinated him because he could never understand how fortune tellers made enough money to run a business. But besides that, there was always something about the little shop that drew him in—something stronger than normal curiosity.

Elliot had walked by it one day and looked in the window. He nearly pressed his face to the glass with childlike amazement as he wondered at all the baubles, crystals, and candles in the store front. There had been a sign in the window that day that said July was the perfect month for card readings due to the position of July's moon. What a perfect opportunity, Elliot thought. If he went on his special day, the reading would be double special then.

Elliot pulled up in front of Madam Mystique's and parked on the street. He walked to the door, umbrella in hand, humming "I'm Singing in the Rain", but he went off by several beats as he grabbed the handle. His mother's voice echoed through his memory telling him that fortune tellers were harlots for the Devil. He rubbed the back of his head and winced. He grabbed the door handle again and his heart thumped. He exhaled and nearly ripped the door open.

Once he entered, he forgot his trepidation as the strong oily aroma of burning incense hit his nostrils. He stumbled for a second as he had never smelled anything like it before. He collapsed his umbrella and leaned it against the door frame in the atrium not wishing to drip water into the shop. He crossed the threshold and stepped into a small square room with faded yellow walls and carpets. The glass counter to his right was filled with octahedron and pyramidal crystals in amethyst, aquamarine, topaz, and lapis lazuli. Next to those were pendulums at the ends of long chains, healing crystals, and meditation spheres all in varying types of quartz.

Elliot looked over his shoulder and his eye was caught by a bookshelf that had all sorts of books about card and palm reading, astrology, astral projection, telekinesis, and rune stones. There were also a number of tarot decks on sale.

Next to the bookshelf was a table with two chairs that faced each other, and on the table was a pot of tea. The sign next to it read "Help Yourself". Elliot poured himself a cup and added a little sugar. It was a unique herbal blend that while smooth, was also a little spicy. Elliot brought the styrofoam cup away from his lips and sighed. His heart was still thumping and his mind raced, but he felt at peace with his decision.

Elliot heard the floorboards creak behind him. He turned and saw a pair of violet curtains behind the glass counter open to reveal a slender woman in her mid-thirties. She had long, curly brown hair and fair skin. Elliot thought she looked very much like a gypsy in her floor-length brown skirt, plain white blouse, and brown bodice with gold stitching.

"Hello!" said Elliot with a smile.

The woman folded her arms. "Good evening. Awfully late, don't you think?"

"Hm? Am I?"

"Are you what?"

"Am I late? Were you expecting me earlier? I mean, fortune telling is your forte."

The woman gave a bemused snicker. "I mean, I don't usually get customers at this time of night."

"Oh, I'm sorry. Are you closed?"

"No…not technically."

They stared at each other for a few seconds.

Elliot sipped his tea. "Delicious!"

"Oh, you like it? My usual patrons tend to think rooibos is a little pedestrian."

"Rooibos? Is that new?"

"No. It's red tea. From South Africa. Has all the benefits of green tea without any of the caffeine."

"Nifty." Elliot sipped again.

The woman paused again. "Can I help you with something?"

"Yes! I came to have my fortune read."

"Oh." The woman relaxed. "You should have said so. I am Madam Mystique."

"How do you do, *Madam Mystique*?" said Elliot dramatically. "I'm Elliot Fraser."

"What kind of fortune did you want?"

"Pardon?"

"Did you want your palm read, a tarot reading, or did you want me to check the stars for you?"

"Well, I'll do whichever you think is best, but I was hoping to do the one with the cards."

"Tarot."

"Yeah!"

"Very well. A reading will be fifty dollars."

Elliot started. "Fifty?! Goodness. So that's how places like this stay in business."

Mystique paused and eyed him.

"But it is a special occasion, so I guess I can splurge a little." Elliot walked over to the counter and pulled out his wallet.

"What's the occasion?"

"It's my birthday!"

"Oh, happy birthday."

"Thank you. I'm thirty-four. I thought it was time I lived a little, so I decided I'd get my fortune read. I've always wanted to!"

Mystique stopped. "This is your idea of living a little?"

"Yes!"

"Not skydiving? Or buying a motorcycle?"

"No, thanks! Too dangerous." Elliot placed fifty dollars on the counter. "Maybe I'll even buy some of these pretty crystals."

"I'm sorry, but we're all out of rose-tinted glasses."

Elliot jumped. "Wow!"

Mystique bit her lip as her eyes widen.

"A place that actually sells rose-tinted glasses! Everyone says that I should buy a pair, but I can't find them anywhere."

Mystique unclenched. "Well then," she said, taking his money. She walked to the back of the store where another set of purple curtains were. "I use a different system than most when it comes to tarot readings. You see, I specialize in tarot. And as a result, I'm a bit of a fanatic."

"Oh, really? I collect bottle caps and stamps myself."

Mystique stopped. She looked over her shoulder.

"And I build model ships! The ones in the bottles are my favorites."

"A-anyway," she said, throwing open the curtains, "welcome to my tarot room."

Elliot gasped as his eyes went wide. Going from the curtain all the way to the back of the store was a room about fifty feet long with three shelves on each side covered in blue velvet with dozens upon dozens of tarot decks lined up.

"It's taken quite a long time to assemble my collection, and it's still nowhere near complete." Mystique turned to him and dropped seven gold coins into his palm. "Pick seven decks from the ones here. Then we'll whittle those down to five, then three, then one. And that will be the one we'll use for your reading."

Elliot entered the hall and turned about. There were so many of them and they each had their own designs. Some were bright, others were dark. Some were simple, others were quite complex. And not all of them had the same amount of cards. Elliot asked about that.

"Some decks only use the major arcana, but most use both the major and minor."

"Does that affect the reading any?"

"Some. But some people tend to think the minor arcana is superfluous."

"How many cards are in a tarot deck?"

"Typically seventy-eight. The minor arcana is made up of fifty-six cards in four suits: swords, cups, coins, and wands. The major arcana is usually twenty-two. But the decks do vary. Anyway, pick the seven that you are most drawn to."

"How will I know if I'm drawn to them?"

"You will know. If you like, I could blindfold you."

"No, thanks. I'll save the piñata for next year."

Mystique furrowed her brow.

Elliot looked down the room slowly. He swallowed. "So many decks. I'll just start right here," he said, dropping a coin on a tall deck with a striped blue background.

The Raider-White Tarot—the old standard.

Elliot walked further along the shelves jingling the coins in his closed hand. He jingled his hand so hard a coin flew out. It landed on the bottom shelf right on top of a deck that had a winged lion.

"Whoops!" Elliot went to pick up the coin. "On second thought, that was probably meant to happen. I'll leave it there."

The Chimera Tarot—despite the inaccurate depiction of the chimera on the back of the cards, the deck was filled with portrait paintings of all sorts of different chimeras. It was a deck meant for those who had a hard time being a single person.

Elliot continued along his way looking at the shelves. "Ooh! 'Anna Strokes.' I had a crush on a girl named Anna in high school. I'll choose that one."

The Anna Strokes Gothic Tarot—a deck meant for lovers of Gothic art, especially fans of the illustrator Anna Strokes, but otherwise it was unremarkable.

"Hmm," said Elliot. "This one looks a little scary, but you only live once."

Mystique jumped. Elliot placed a coin on a deck that had what looked like a shadow figure on it. It was the Mortujuricodex Tarot—a deck specifically meant to aid mediums in communicating with the dead. It could be used to decipher the lives of the dearly departed or even be used as a means of connecting with and banishing them. A warlock from a death cult was the impetus for the creation of that deck.

"Hmm, this man is holding a book on this card. I like books."

The Grimoire Tarot—based on the short story of the same name by E.A. Wellscraft, a horror writer who lived in the late Victorian period. The pictures in the deck were comprised of scenes from his most famous work.

"Ooh! This one seems all right. It reminds me of those two faces that are associated with drama and the theatre. My mother loves the theatre."

"It's actually more based on the yin-yang symbol. Each face is a different color with the eyes being the opposite color."

"Oh, yes. I see."

The Persona Tarot—a heartwarming deck meant for people who often have complex and deep friendships.

"Okay, just one more," directed Mystique.

"Hmm." Elliot wandered the room, going up and down the shelves multiple times. "There are a lot of nifty ones, but none of them really speak to me."

Mystique checked her watch. "Don't dawdle now."

"Is it close to closing time?"

"No… I technically don't close. But still, please don't keep me."

"Doesn't it cost a lot of money to be open all hours of the day?"

"I have some…irregular customers."

"What interesting people they must be to want a tarot reading in the middle of the night."

"Not really," Mystique mumbled under her breath. They were usually a bunch of nuts willing to pay top dollar for readings, even if that meant a three hundred percent surcharge for getting Mystique out of bed.

After another five minutes, Elliot shrugged. "I can't decide," he said with a smile. "I guess I'll go with this basic black one."

Mystique gasped. The color drained from her face. The Black Tarot. "Are you s-sure about that one?"

"Sure! Why not?"

"Y-you're a hundred percent certain?"

"Yes!"

Mystique began to sweat. "Very well… Please wait here. I need to get something."

She quickly went to her other backroom to fetch a cart on which the decks would be displayed. But as she grabbed the cart, her hands shook. The Black Tarot—that deck had only one purpose, and in all the years she had been a fortune teller, no one had ever asked for a reading from it. Even the most wretched and abysmal people to walk through her door were averse to its presence. And yet, Elliot placed a coin on it like it was no big deal.

But then reason began to come over her. She shook her head. A person like Elliot wouldn't notice its aura. And what were the chances that he'd choose it over any of the other six?

But, just to be safe, Mystique grabbed a pair of white gloves and a tub of warm water to purify the negative energy from the coin that touched the deck. She wheeled the cart back to the deck room.

"Alright. I'll put the decks on the cart and we'll go into the other room, and you can whittle down your choices."

"Sounds great. Do you want some help?"

"No. Wait! Yes. I would *love* some help. Why don't you grab that last deck you chose?"

"Sure." Elliot scooped up the deck without a problem.

Mystique started to sweat again.

"What's the tub of water for?"

"Oh, that's, um, to cleanse the energies off the coins. Everything you touch leaves behind a piece of your aura. And to keep the readings as pure as possible, I try to keep the coins as pure as possible."

"I see. Should I go ahead and toss this coin in there then?"

"Um…" Mystique paused. Elliot had touched the deck without a problem. He had even smiled while he moved it.

"Madam Mystique?"

"Huh? Oh. Uh, tell you what, sport: since this is your first reading and your birthday, why don't you go ahead and keep that coin."

"Wow! For real?!"

"Certainly."

"Great. Thanks!" Elliot dropped the coin into his pocket. "I'll get some of the other decks."

Mystique almost shrieked. "No! I mean, that is, please take a seat in the other room. Try to relax and focus your mind. Try to focus on what questions you have."

"Um, okay." Elliot shot her a quick look as he exited.

After a couple more minutes, Mystique came back to the table with all seven decks—the other six placed a good distance away from the Black Tarot.

"Very well, then. Please choose five from these seven."

"Hmm…"

Mystique found herself praying to any god that would answer.

"Well, this one kind of scares me, so that's out, and I'm really not into fantasy, so this one is out, too."

Mystique grabbed the Mortujuricodex and Chimera Tarots and put them on a lower shelf of the cart.

"A-alright. Now, please choose three."

"Well, as much as I love the theatre, I'm not really into this one, and this one's a little boring."

Mystique's heart began to pound as she removed the Persona and Raider-White Tarots. "Now, p-please ch-choose one."

"Hmm." Elliot went back and forth between the Anna Strokes, the Grimoire, and Black Tarots.

Mystique hoped he was secretly a lover of Gothic artwork.

"Hmm, well, I think…I'm going to go with the lonely one over here."

Mystique's heart seized. "A-are you s-s-sure?!"

"Yes. Quite certain. I said my goodbyes to Anna when I went to college. And the one with the book looks a little predictable. The black one over here just seems so lonely. It's calling out to me. It says, 'I wanna be your friend!' Can you hear it? If you listen real close, you can almost hear it."

Mystique choked. She had stopped breathing from shock due to Elliot's childish joke. "Um, are you absolutely, positively sure you want to use that deck?"

"Yes. Does it have a name?"

"Some call it..." Mystique swallowed. "The Black Tarot."

"Really? That's kind of lame, but it is fitting."

A crack of thunder went off as rain pelted the windows.

Elliot shivered. "Huh. I just got chills. So, how about that reading?"

"S-sure." Mystique tripped, trying to sit down.

"Are you all right?"

"Fine," she said in a tiny voice. "Um…why don't you go ahead and shuffle the deck, and think about your question."

"Okay." Elliot set the deck on the table and began to shuffle. "Are you all right? You look pale."

"I'm fine." Mystique tried to calm herself. Okay, so he chose the deck, but that didn't mean it would respond to him. There was still a chance.

She steadied her hand, still gloved, and took the deck from Elliot. "So, what's your question?"

Elliot shrugged. "I just want to know my fortune."

"Usually that means a reading about the future."

"Like will I win the lottery or find love?"

"Yes."

"Ooh! Can't wait!"

Mystique placed the deck in front of her and as she went to draw the top card, she tried to make up her mind about which spread to use. To offset the deck, she would try the Celtic cross spread despite the fact the deck was made to be read in only one way—the inverted pentagram spread.

She drew the first card and placed it in the center of the spread which represented the matter at hand. It depicted a man dancing at the edge of a sheer cliff while a squat demon played a flute luring him closer. Mystique received a vision of a man choosing to ignore the people whispering around him.

Mystique drew the second card and put it on top of the first horizontally, making up the center of the cross. This card represented forces hindering the matter. It depicted a man in simple and dirty clothing as he carried a message in his hand. A dark cloud was above his head, but he was oblivious to it. Mystique received a second vision of a man being guilted by several authority figures of different genders into making decisions he didn't want to make.

Mystique was confused. She cast a look at Elliot.

"What is it?"

"I-It's just…the Servant."

"And?"

"Like I said earlier, not all tarot decks have the same cards or even the same number. This deck is unusual in that while it has most of the major arcana used in other tarots, it also has some unique major arcana. The Servant is one of them."

"What does it mean?"

"It's a representation of someone who serves blissfully, ignorantly, or isn't in control of his own will."

"What was the first one?"

"The Fool. He represents carefree ignorance."

"Hmm," said Elliot in a concerned tone. "I hope this all works out."

"Me, too," she said in a breathy whisper.

Mystique drew the third card, representing underlying influences, and placed it below the center cards making the bottom of the cross. She laid down a card of a house burning and an image flashed through her head. She saw a small, old farm house set against the night sky. It was completely engulfed in flames and crackling. Mystique rubbed her head.

"Are you alright?"

"Fine…"

"So, which card is that?"

Mystique composed herself. "The Tower. Drastic and sudden change. Often unfortunate."

Elliot's eyebrows rose.

Mystique drew the fourth card, influences that are coming to an end, and placed it to the left of the center. She laid it down and felt relieved to see the hooded skeleton. But then her relief left as she had a vision of a man, beaten and bloody, burning to death.

Elliot freaked out. "What is that?!"

"C-Calm down! It's just Death."

Elliot bristled.

"It doesn't mean as in someone is going to die. I mean, it could, but usually it just means change. You know, when your situation changes, it's sort of like the death of the old situation."

Elliot still looked alarmed.

Mystique was also alarmed. The spread didn't seem to make sense. What sort of changing influences was Elliot going through that could be coming to an end? And how was the Tower mixed up in it? She wanted to stop, but she felt compelled to press on.

Mystique drew the fifth card, influences that may become important, and put it above the center. It turned out to be the image of a handsome man with a head of curly blond hair. He had angelic wings, but half of his face was distorted. Mystique gasped. Her vision returned, and the man went from being on fire to standing over four others, all of which were dead, their blood covering the man.

Elliot looked at Mystique but didn't say anything.

Mystique drew the sixth card, influences on the questioner in the near future. This one would go to the right of the center, and the cross would be complete.

She laid it down and saw a serpentine face with red eyes and rows of sharp teeth, smiling wickedly at her. There was a blood curdling roar in her mind and her body went cold. She screamed and everything went dark.

Mystique awoke to find herself on the shop floor. Her hip and head hurt, and Elliot kept calling her name.

"Madam Mystique! Madam Mystique! Are you all right?"

She sat up. "Ariola," she groaned.

"Huh?"

"Ariola. My name's Ariola."

"Oh. Um, are you all right?"

"I think—" But then her heart seized and her chest rose as a sharp pain hit her head as another vision came. She saw the burning house again, and a man walked out of it holding his arm. A black serpentine shape emerged out of the night sky and turned into a dragon with red eyes. It roared and the house collapsed. Somebody screamed.

She panted.

"Ariola?! What is it?"

She looked at him out of the corner of her eye. She pulled her knees up to her chin and wrapped her arms around them. "Look, I have to be honest with you. The Black Tarot has another name. It's called…Tarot Draconis, Filius Satanae. It's Latin for 'The Tarot of the Dragon.'" Ariola looked at Elliot. "'The Son of Satan.'"

Elliot was silent for a few seconds. He tried to make words, but his mouth wouldn't move. Finally, he said, "What? What are you talking about?"

"This tarot was made for the explicit purpose of predicting the coming of the Dragon, the Son of Satan, and to be used by him…during his reign of terror."

Elliot's eyes darted back and forth. His mouth was agape. But after a few tense seconds, he laughed.

Ariola stared at him.

"Whoo! What a story! I've got to tell you, Ariola—er, I mean, *Madam Mystique*," he said dramatically again. "This has been quite a night. You really went all out. If my mother was here, she'd say, 'See, Elliot?! I told you all fortune tellers are evil!' Then she'd slap me upside the head!" He laughed again. Then rubbed the back of his head and cringed.

"This isn't a joke! Look!" Ariola stood. "Look at the cards!" Ariola stopped. "What the hell…?"

"What's the matter?"

"Th-The shape…"

"The shape of what?"

"The spread. The shape of the spread!"

"Yeah," said Elliot dumbfounded. "It's a star."

"No! It can't be." Ariola stepped back. "I was doing the Celtic cross. I made a cross with the first six cards!" She looked at Elliot with wide eyes. "Didn't I?"

Elliot looked at her. "No," he said, shaking his head. "You laid them out in a star."

"B-But how? I couldn't have…" Ariola's hand went up to her head. Had it all been an illusion? Had the deck tricked her?!

Ariola looked down at the spread. She looked at the cards, their placement in the spread, and her vision began to make sense.

"What is it?" asked Elliot.

"I performed the inverted pentagram spread."

"So?"

"It's the Satanic Star! This is the only spread that can be used with this tarot. I tried using a different spread—I *saw* myself using a different spread—but the deck tricked me and forced me to use this one!"

Elliot gave her a pitying look. Then he smiled. "You really don't have to carry on like this. I'm amused. Really, I am."

"Look! The first position, the top left point representing the past. The Fool, carefree ignorance."

"And?"

"Describes you perfectly! The second position, bottom left point is the present. The Servant, one who doesn't know his own will. The third position, bottom point is the immediate future. The Tower, tragedy. The fifth position, top right point is hidden influences. Lucifer! *Lucifer*! Enlightenment and unholy benediction."

"How can benediction be unholy?"

"And the final position, the center, the future on the current path, the Dragon! The Dragon! The Son of Satan!"

"And what about the fourth card? The bottom right point?"

"Possible future on an opposing path, Death. Either as in change or actual death."

Elliot regarded the cards. "Okay… So, what does it mean?"

Ariola sighed and collapsed into her chair. "It should be pretty obvious."

Elliot's eyebrows rose. "You're saying…I'm the Dragon? I'm the Son of the Devil?!"

"Seems so…"

"Can't be."

Ariola shook her head. "What?"

"I'm not a fool and I'm not a servant. I know exactly who I am, what I'm doing, and where I'm going!"

Ariola shook. "Do you?!"

"Yes! I am Elliot Fraser. Thirty-four. Six-foot-three, white male. I'm a computer programmer for Vitech where I just got a promotion thanks to all the hard work I do, and I live in Clinton Township."

"And what's that supposed to mean?"

"I am the result of all my own choices. They were good choices. The right choices. No one's controlling me."

"Really? Tell me: what are your dreams?"

"My dreams?"

"Yes. What's something you've always wanted or wanted to do?"

Elliot thought for a minute. "I'd always wanted my fortune told."

"That's pathetic!"

"You talk that way about your own trade?"

"You don't dream of getting a card reading. You get one to make sure you're on the right path, and if not, how to change your path. No one aspires to one day sit in the chair opposite me. There must be something else. *Anything* else."

Elliot sat down; he was quiet for a while.

"Really? Nothing?! There's not anything else in the whole world you want?"

Elliot mumbled a response.

Ariola cocked her head. "Say that again."

Elliot mumbled louder.

"Did you say, 'friends?'"

Elliot looked down. "Nobody likes me. And I don't know why. I've tried all my life to be friendly and sociable, but people either ignore me or make fun of me behind my back. They have no respect for me and even make fun of me to my face."

Elliot put his head on his hand. "In truth though…" he began, "I want it all," he said with hunger. "Friends, money, power, women… I want everything."

"What's stopping you?"

Elliot gave a hopeless shrug. "I'm Elliot Fraser. I'm a thirty-four year old computer programmer for the crummiest company in the industry. I only took the job so I could be close to my mother and take care of her. Which I only did because she guilted me into it. Said she would die if I moved out. Add to that, my hobbies are boring, I never do anything I actually enjoy. Women cringe at the sight of me; my bosses think I'm incompetent and a pushover."

"But you said you got a promotion."

"Yeah, because I've been putting in a lot of work because I haven't had a weekend off in six months. They thought that since I was there all the time I could do more work. They gave me a special computer that can access the most important systems and programs, but it's horribly dull work. Dull, dull, dull!

"My life…" Elliot stopped, but he looked like he was trying to say a word.

Ariola thought it may have started with an S. She ventured, "Sucks?"

"Yes! Geez. I'm too scared to even swear." Elliot rubbed the back of his head again.

"I see," said Ariola.

Elliot sighed. "This is the first decent conversation I've had with a person since…I can't even remember when."

Elliot was quiet for a while. He leaned over the table and picked up the Fool. "The Fool, huh? Yeah, that sounds like me. I try my damnedest to stay in the dark about how pathetic my life really is because the more I look at it, the less I like it." He put the Fool down. Then he spun the Dragon around with his finger. "What is the Dragon?"

"He's the Son of Satan."

"But what does that mean?"

"The Dragon is pure evil and brings great suffering with him wherever he goes. He makes Hell on Earth."

"Okay, but what does that actually mean? What evil does he cause?"

Ariola shrugged. "All of it? Rape, murder, theft, human sacrifice. Blasphemy? I don't know. He's the ultimate villain."

"I see."

Elliot swiveled the card back and forth a little. It made Ariola's skin crawl.

"Is there any way of confirming that I'm the Dragon?"

"What do you mean? That's what the tarot was made for. It was made to predict the advent of the Dragon and to be used by him during his conquest."

"Is that truly what the cards are saying though?"

Ariola stared at him. "What do you mean?"

"Well, you're a card reader. Is there any way to see further into the future? Or to confirm this?"

"I can draw another card and see if it offers any hints…" Ariola did so and she dropped it next to the Dragon. The image was of a woman in shackles, wearing black robes that barely draped around her body, leaving her bust exposed. "Huh. The Oracle."

"What does it mean?"

"It just means 'future events'. It's one of those cards that doesn't mean anything by itself. But I have no idea what it could mean." Ariola looked up at Elliot, and the second their eyes met, a shiver went down her spine.

Elliot looked down at the spread, but after a beat, he stood up. "Well, I think I should be going. Mom has to take her pills before she goes to bed, and she'll beat my ass if I don't remind her. Good night." Elliot grabbed his umbrella and disappeared into the storm.

Ariola was very confused. It wasn't every day someone hears he's the Devil's progeny and then just walks off as if they had just been wished a good morning. Elliot had seemed worried and disgusted before, but now, he didn't seem to care. Why? What made him change his mind so suddenly?

Ariola stared at the Oracle. She really didn't like it. Somewhere in her mind, she heard glass shattering and a woman screaming. She felt as if something had "arms" around her—they were cold. She felt trapped, abused, and scared. She felt violated, but couldn't figure out why or in what way.

Dark Ascension

Elliot's drive home was quiet. Usually he listened to the radio preferring soft rock or adult contemporary, but everything Ariola had said stuck with him. The idea that he could be the son of Satan and commit heinous acts of evil seemed beyond him. But something about it was appealing. Ariola had called the Dragon the ultimate villain, and villains always had everything they could ever want: money, power, women, and people feared them. All of that would be a nice change of pace.

Elliot pulled up to his house in Clinton Township. His home had once been an old farm. It hadn't been very big, but they still retained some of the land from the old days making their property at least twice the size of any of their neighbors'. The lawn was neatly trimmed, but some of the bushes were overgrown. And though the house was old and small and needed to be painted, it was still architecturally sound.

Elliot pulled his car into the unpaved drive and noticed something strange as he got out—all the lights in the house were off. His mother couldn't have gone to bed already, it was too early. And it was very strange that the porch light hadn't been turned on.

He opened the front door into the darkened living room. He expected to see his mother lounging on the couch watching old movies, but she wasn't there. He looked into their connecting dining room and kitchen, but both were dark and completely empty.

Elliot turned to close the door when he noticed something odd. The birthday cake he had bought for himself had a piece missing. He had cut one for himself and one for his mother, which she refused so he ate it anyway, and that had been it. But as he looked at the small sheet cake, there was quite a bit of it missing and it didn't look like someone had cut it, but rather just grabbed it with a bare hand.

There was a creak behind Elliot, but before he could turn, an aluminum bat cracked him across the back of the head. He dropped instantly.

Elliot awoke to find himself on the floor of his bedroom on the second floor with his hands tied behind him. He had a splitting headache and there were several other slight aches and pains all over his body—he had a vague recollection of being dragged up a rough incline. Then he became aware of several figures in his room. At least four were men and there was one short, rotund shape that continued to whimper like a beaten dog.

One of the men bent over and peered at Elliot. "He's awake."

"Finally," a second laughed. "Hold this old bitch, Dan."

A man stepped to the side and grabbed the woman.

The second man stepped up and Elliot tried to roll over so he could see him, but his face was still shrouded by the darkness of the house.

"Hello, Elliot," said the man. "Miss me?"

"Miss…you? Who are you?"

"Who am I?! You mean to tell me you don't recognize me?"

"I can't see your face…"

"But you don't even recognize my voice. We used to work together at the same shitty company. Remember Vitech? Oh, wait, that's right. *You* still work there."

Elliot was confused. He tried to remember working with someone who had left recently, but his mind was still foggy from the bat to the head. "I'm sorry…"

"It's me…Robert."

Elliot's eyes went wide. "Robert Adelstein?!"

"That's right. Now, you remember."

"Yes, I remember you. You were fired for stealing."

"I was fired because of you!"

"You downloaded a virus into accounting's system to commit penny shaving."

"So? Vitech never would've noticed the missing money."

"Not at first, but eventually. And it wouldn't have taken them long to figure out when the programming was changed by calculating how much money had gone missing and how slowly the account was growing, and then simply working backward from there."

"By that time, I would be in Tahiti with hundreds of thousands of dollars at my disposal. They never would have found me."

"Really?" said Elliot indignantly. "Well, that might be true, but the fact that I noticed a glitch in the programming a few days after you uploaded it shows how sloppy you were. And I'm not very good at my job to begin with." Elliot smiled, amused. It was his first real smile in decades.

"And *you* just had to go and tell somebody. Couldn't leave it alone, couldn't ignore it?!" Adelstein kicked Elliot in the ribs.

Elliot coughed. "I was just doing my job…"

"'Just doing my job,'" mocked Adelstein. He kicked Elliot again.

"What are you doing here, Robert? You're supposed to be in prison."

"I felt that the institution didn't have anything else to offer. And so, I'm here," Adelstein crouched down, "for some good, old-fashioned revenge."

Elliot was quiet for a second. Then he laughed.

Adelstein growled. "What's so funny?"

"You've got some real…*shit* for brains!" replied Elliot.

His mother wailed. He had never really sworn before.

His heart beat quickly and his mind raced. "You're going to take revenge on me. Well, go ahead…*asshole*! I haven't got anything worth stealing, and honestly, my life isn't worth anything to anyone. Not even me."

"Oh, we can't have that," said Adelstein as he stood. He placed his foot on Elliot's head. "Maybe you'll change your mind when you and your fat, bitchy mother are charring to a crisp! But first, we're going to help ourselves to your work computer. I heard through the grapevine that you have access to all the major systems at Vitech."

Elliot's eyes went wide again.

"Right…Grant?"

"Grant?! You're working for Robert?!"

"*With* Robert," said the last man. "I'm sorry, Elliot. But we would've cut you in on the deal if you had just kept your mouth shut."

"Ugh! Grant, you asshole."

"Hey," said Adelstein, "when did this guy grow a sack?"

Grant shrugged.

"Well, whatever. Jerry, you keep Elliot company."

"Can I treat him to my special brand of hospitality?" laughed Jerry as he pounded his fist into his hand.

"Sure! I bet you could even cut the zip tie holding his wrists together and he still wouldn't fight back. He's a real pussy."

"I love an easy fight."

Adelstein and Jerry laughed.

Adelstein, Dan, and Grant took Elliot's wailing mother with them as they left.

Jerry advanced on Elliot. "You and I are going to have some fun." Jerry pulled Elliot to his feet by the collar, held him against the wall, and started punching him in the face.

Elliot had never been in a fight before. Each strike brought on a dull impact followed by a sting and he started to lose his ambition to resist.

Jerry cracked Elliot across the jaw. Elliot faced Jerry and spat blood in his face.

"Now, we're talkin'," said Jerry. He continued to beat Elliot, punching and kneeing him in the stomach.

Somewhere on the ground floor, Elliot could hear his mother screaming as someone told her to shut up and the others ransacked the house. There was a smacking sound through the floor followed by a heavy thud—his mother was quiet.

Jerry slugged Elliot in the nose and blood was summoned in its wake. He threw all of his weight into a jab across Elliot's face and knocked him into the antique wardrobe next to him. Elliot's head smashed into the edge and he fell.

Jerry exhaled. "Robbie wasn't kidding. You don't fight back. I never noticed before, but I actually like it when my prey resists a little. I bet I *could* beat you without your hands tied behind your back."

Jerry pulled out a chair in Elliot's room and sat in it. He put his arm on the table next to it and quickly pulled it back up. "What is this shit?!" Jerry leaned closer to the table top. "Bottle caps and stamps?" He looked back at Elliot on the floor. "What a fucking loser." Jerry knocked it all onto the floor.

Suddenly, there was screaming from the ground floor again. Someone lost shouted, "Shut up, you stupid bitch!" There was another smack followed by more wailing.

Elliot could barely hear anything. He was so far away in his own realm of pain that nothing else mattered. But there was something, far in the back of his mind, that began to grow. Death—not the word, but the image of a hooded skeleton. The hooded skeleton went from being a piece of line art to a real figure as it stood over the body of a man, bruised and bleeding, as fire started to envelop him. The vision was followed by an explanation: "Possible future…"

Elliot heard a deep voice. "Do you want to die?"

"No," Elliot replied.

"You are going to die."

"I don't want to die."

"Then you must fight."

"I don't want to fight."

"'I don't want to fight. I'm a good boy.' Pathetic. Wretched. Abysmal. You're a loser, Elliot Fraser, and you're going to die a loser's death."

"Shut up!"

"What?" said Jerry, jumping.

"I'm not going to die," said Elliot through grit teeth.

"Why not?"

"Because I want to live. Today, I did something I've never done before and I was…"

"Liberated. You loved the rush and exhilaration of doing something you've always wanted."

"Yes!"

"You want to always feel that way."

"Yes!"

"Money, power, women—those will liberate you. Is that what you think?"

"Well…"

"What the hell did you say?" asked Jerry, standing.

"Do you truly want those things? Do you truly desire liberation?"

123

"...Yes. I want to be free. I want money, power, and women... I want it all. I want everything..." Elliot looked up. "And most of all..."

"Hmm...?"

"I want to be feared!"

Jerry laughed. "I ain't scared of you, you shitless wonder."

"Then you know what you must do. Become the Dragon... Take these four wretches before you... They will be the test to see if you're worthy of being feared. Their blood will liberate you! Show them your fury, show them your strength, show them they are right to be scared of you! Become the Dragon."

"I...am..."

"Hey!" shouted Jerry. "What the fuck are you on about?" Jerry picked Elliot up. "You think you're big and bad, now?"

Elliot lifted his head and made eye contact. Jerry recoiled slightly—this wasn't the same guy he had been beating. But it didn't matter, he was still beat.

"You're not bad!" Jerry shoved Elliot into the wall. "I've hit you so hard you're imagining things. Hell, I think we're about done here." Jerry took a switchblade out of his pocket and opened it. He grabbed Elliot by the chin and pulled his own arm back.

"Why don't you untie my hands and see for yourself?"

"What was that?"

"I said, untie my hands and let's see who's actually bad."

"Oh, really?" Jerry laughed. "That's funny."

"Laugh it up...wretch!"

Elliot surged forward and headbutt Jerry as hard as he could. Jerry dropped his knife, stumbled back, and cursed. Elliot squatted and cut the zip tie. He raised the knife and went to stab Jerry.

Jerry looked up in time and grabbed Elliot's wrist. Elliot went to punch him, but Jerry wrapped his arm around Elliot's. Jerry kneed Elliot in the groin and he doubled over, dropping the switchblade. Jerry grabbed Elliot by the chin and landed a solid punch on him. Jerry pulled back for a second, but Elliot landed an uppercut into Jerry's groin. Jerry howled and doubled over.

Elliot took the offensive grabbing Jerry and whirled him around, smashing him into the wardrobe. Elliot swung him around the other way and Jerry tripped over Elliot's bed, smacking his head into one of the posters.

Elliot grabbed Jerry by the collar and pulled him up, but Jerry punched him in the nose. Elliot crashed over his table, his hand landing on a glass cylinder. Jerry got up and went for another punch, but Elliot turned at the last minute and shattered the glass bottle, model ship and all, into Jerry's face.

Jerry clutched his bleeding face and moaned. He cursed, swearing he was going to get Elliot, but Elliot slipped behind him and forced Jerry's head forward and down, smashing it into one of the table's corners. There was a crack and a sudden stop, and Jerry went limp.

Something dark cheered.

Elliot took a step back. He stood as tall as he could and wiped the blood from his face.

Adelstein's voice came from below. "Jesus! What's going on up there? Go check it out, Dan."

"I…am…" said Elliot.

Heavy footsteps ran up the stairs.

Elliot quickly reached over to his worktable and picked up a modeling knife with a razor sharp blade.

Dan made it to the room and looked through the doorway. He first saw Elliot just standing there. Then he saw Jerry with the table's corner embedded into his head.

"Jerry!" Dan looked back up at Elliot. "You motherfucker!"

Dan charged, but Elliot struck like a viper, embedding the knife into Dan's skull with all his strength. He pushed Dan against the doorframe and worked the knife into his head, but Dan wouldn't die—the point of the modeling knife was too short.

Dan screamed and struggled. He pulled his fist back for a punch, but Elliot replied by repeatedly stabbing Dan in the head and face. Dan screamed louder.

Elliot tried to silence him by stabbing the modeling knife into his throat over and over. Dan's yells gurgled. He tried to stop Elliot, but Elliot was bigger.

Then with a slight adjustment to his hand and arm, Elliot went from stabbing Dan in the neck to slashing him across the throat. He ended the combo by embedding the modeling knife halfway up its handle into Dan's eye socket.

Dan stopped thrashing and slid down the door frame.

A phantom laughed.

Elliot stepped into the hall. He didn't hear anything from downstairs. Grant and Adelstein had heard the scuffle, and if they didn't hear from Dan soon, they would realize what happened.

Elliot descended the stairs with singular focus. Everything his eyes fell upon burned and shriveled up. Fury radiated off him, giving him an unnatural aura as if light bent around him so that it wouldn't have to touch him, making the space around him darker than anywhere else.

He reached the first floor and turned into the living room. There was a whooshing sound and Elliot ducked under the baseball bat. He punched Grant in the face, ducked another wild swing, and elbowed Grant across the temple.

Grant fell, dropping the bat. He looked around wildly and tried to grab it, but Elliot stepped and crushed Grant's hand with his heel. Grant yelled.

Elliot kicked Grant across the face. He was thrown back into the coffee table, knocking his head against it. He shook the pain off, but as he went to get up, the end of the baseball bat stroked the side of his head.

Grant looked up at Elliot and saw a man not wholly there, completely apathetic to the situation.

"What sort of monster are you?"

"I am…the…"

Elliot's dead gaze held Grant's long enough until the bat was inches from his head. There was nothing he could do as it collided into his temple, knocking him to the side. He went to get up but another whack to the back of the head stopped him. There was another one and this one was followed by a vicious crack.

Elliot dropped the bat next to Grant's body as he wandered into the kitchen. He turned and saw Adelstein with a butcher's knife to his mother's throat.

Adelstein's voice quavered. "Wha…What the fuck?!"

Elliot just stood there. He looked less like a man, and more like a spirit that had just manifested. He was as grim as a shadow and twice as eerie. But Adelstein wouldn't be made a fool of.

"I'm going to kill this old lady!"

"Go ahead." Elliot's voice was hollow and distant. "She was never my mother."

"Elliot!" his mother wailed. "What're you saying?"

"She hated me. She hated me before she knew me. I was the cause of all her pain. I'm the reason her man left. She turned her pain into mine, the child she would've gladly given up to have him back. But she stuck with me out of a misguided sense of moral virtue rather than smothering me in my sleep like she wanted."

"Elliot!" his mother wailed. "Stop it!"

"I remember how you used to come into my room with a pillow in your hands and the bathtub running… It would've been easy to make it look like a tragic accident."

"Elliot!"

Adelstein shook. He looked at the old woman. He clenched her tighter and poked the knife harder against her throat. "I'm serious!"

"Go ahead… I have no mother."

Adelstein tensed up. "Give me your work computer and this'll all be over, Elliot!"

"You mean this one?" said Elliot, picking up a messenger bag right next to the front door. "The computer that will allow you access into Vitech's systems and files, and let you raise all the havoc you want?"

"That's right." Adelstein held out his hand.

"There's a problem with it."

"What's that?"

Elliot dropped the bag on the floor and drove his heel into it. There was a crunch. "It's broken."

"Sonuva bitch! If you had just given it to me, I wouldn't have to kill you both now."

Elliot paused. He lifted his hand and flexed it into a fist. "Two of us will die, but neither will be me."

"Oh yeah, motherfucker?!" Adelstein ripped the butcher's knife across the old woman's throat. In a flash of red, there was a scream. He charged Elliot, but Elliot managed to evade him as if he wasn't totally there. Adelstein spun, whirling the knife as dangerously as he could. The blade bit into Elliot's temple, but Elliot managed to grab Adelstein's arm and trap it. He ripped his fist across Adelstein's face before pulling it back and doing it again and again.

Adelstein's nose bled as he slumped over, but he didn't fall as Elliot still held him. He punched Elliot in the groin, and Elliot let go, retreating. Adelstein charged and tackled Elliot into the kitchen, pinning him against a counter.

The two wrestled, bashing each other against the counters and appliances, smashing dishes and cabinets as they went. Adelstein kicked Elliot back, but Elliot rebounded with a tackle. Adelstein moved to the side and grabbed something out of the corner of his eye. He ripped it across the back of Elliot's head and the milk bottle shattered, drenching Elliot.

Elliot slumped on the counter. He was worn out. He could hardly see, and blood leaked from his nose and mouth.

Adelstein pulled another knife from the kitchen's block and drove it into Elliot's upper arm. The searing pain brought Elliot back to life and he spun, grabbed Adelstein's groin, and squeezed and twisted. Adelstein howled, dropping the knife, but he managed to reach into his waistband and draw a small revolver.

There was a shot.

The stinging pain in Adelstein's crotch ceased as Elliot fell to the floor.

Adelstein slumped backwards into a kitchen counter. He laughed nervously. "Hell of a fight, but in the end, I win!" Adelstein started to dance, but the pain between his legs stopped him. "Aw, fuck! I should get the hell out of here anyway."

He went to the living room and picked up a gas can. He began splashing it around the ground floor when his foot tapped the messenger bag. He picked it up. "Even if the computer is damaged, all the data should be intact." He dropped the gas can and walked back over to Elliot—he wasn't moving.

Adelstein took his gun out again. "Just to make sure."

Suddenly, there was a noise that was like a cross between a belch and a moan. It sent shivers down Adelstein's spine. He turned and didn't see anyone, but the room was suddenly very cold, reeked of brimstone, and he had the distinct impression he wasn't alone.

Then he felt something sharp pierce his neck. He jumped but something held him down. He tried to turn, but he was kicked in the back of the leg and the back of his head was brought down backward into something hard. His mind went fuzzy and something hard slammed into his back. It took some effort, but he realized he was on the ground, and someone was standing over him.

Adelstein looked up at Elliot, blood dripping from his side. "Who…" Adelstein wheezed. "Who the fuck are you?"

A humorless grin stretched over Elliot's face. "I am…the Dragon."

Adelstein felt a chill shoot through his body as flames erupted all over him. He screamed.

Consummation

Elliot was outside. He was on his knees on the front lawn. He held his arm as it still bled. The house behind him was roaring and crackling as it burned, giving off an intense heat.

Sirens announced the arrival of EMS vehicles, including an ambulance, a fire truck, and several police cars.

A fire fighter went up to Elliot. "Hey, buddy! Are you all right?"

Elliot looked up slowly.

The fire fighter jumped back.

Elliot smiled. "I'm fine."

"Who…who are you?"

"I am…"

But he was interrupted by screams coming from inside the house. A woman's voice was calling out for Elliot. A few of the fire fighters rushed to the side of the house in fireproof gear, looking for a way in.

Elliot stood and began to walk away.

"Sir!" said an EMT. "Are you Elliot?"

The screaming intensified. The EMT looked at the house.

Elliot turned his head to the side and spat. The front half of the house collapsed and the screaming ceased.

There was a roar as the flames blazed more fiercely, and Elliot left the panicking first responders behind.

The Occult Killer

On the west side of Detroit was a rundown apartment building. One of the apartments was furnished with only a dirty and torn up couch along with a large, old television. A scrawny man in a worn out, button-down shirt one size too big for him and dirty jeans sat on the couch and sharpened a katana with the tip of the blade embedded in the floor. A cross dangled from his neck as he leaned over the red-stained blade, dragging a whetstone across it. The only light source in the room was coming from the TV.

"And in other news," said the reporter, "on the east side of Detroit in the city of Roseville, a small business was ransacked late last night."

The man looked up from his sword.

"The shop was Madam Mystique's Fantastical Emporium run by local woman, thirty-four year old Ariola Lenormand. She specializes in selling good luck crystals and telling fortunes. She's famous for her expansive tarot deck collection and allowing clients to choose which deck they would like to have their fortunes read from.

"Police believe the shop was broken into sometime after midnight. There was evidence of a struggle but nothing appears to be stolen except for a single tarot deck. Police attempted to contact Miss Lenormand, but have had difficulty doing so and now believe she is being held against her will. There are no suspects at this time.

"If you have any information on the suspect or the whereabouts of Miss Lenormand, you are encouraged to contact Roseville police.

"In other news, a home in Clinton Township burned to the ground earlier last night where five bodies were iden—"

The man shut off the TV. He inspected the edge on his katana. He held up a sheet of loose leaf paper and the katana sheared it with ease. The man smirked and sheathed it.

He put on a large, black overcoat. "Looks like I'm not the only one who's trying to clean up this town."

The man picked up his katana and exited out the window. He climbed down the fire escape to access the street below.

"Destroy all that is evil, so that good may flourish."

END OF TALES OF HORROR VOL. I

SEE YOU NEXT TIME, PHOBOPHILIACS

Coming Attractions

Feature 1

    Chrissy returned to her quarters. She didn't care what Tim said—she was still excited to meet Dr. Dorian, even if he had become fond of the drink in recent years. He was still a renowned marine zoologist, credited with helping to develop underwater technology and helping to further research on the psychic abilities of marine animals.
    Still though, as Chrissy proceeded to sit on her bed and open her computer, she couldn't push all the stories and rumors from her mind. Drinking was only one of them, and not even the worst at that. For the past ten years, he had also spent his life chasing sea monsters and sea serpent stories. Some even said he was part of an investigation on Lake Superior in the state of Michigan. The story went that they were looking for a sea monster that had killed everyone except for Dr. Dorian. That was even supposed to be the reason why he had helped develop the underwater technology they currently used—to find sea monsters.
    Chrissy didn't know much more than that. But ever since she had studied Dr. Dorian in grad school, she never allowed anything anyone say tarnish his image in her mind. She looked up to him, and no one, not even Tim, could take that from her.
    Chrissy set to her work and overlooked the bioscanner reports of the types of fish that swam past the facility and the surrounding areas. Maybe she'd finally see her first giant squid, or perhaps identify the anomaly they kept picking up farther out.
    As she worked, Chrissy turned on the imaging dome above her. Despite that no sunlight reached the bottom of the Pacific Ocean, the software would pick up whatever was directly outside, brighten it up, and broadcast it for her to see if she looked up. She also preferred the soft blue glow of the ocean than her room's fluorescent bulbs, not to mention the added bonus of possibly seeing something unique outside should she see an interesting shadow cast around her room.
    Chrissy began documenting the types of fish. Thanks to the bioscanners, she could pick up recordings in real time and a few began coming through. In zone seven, there was a report of an angler fish while in zone two there were

several reports of tripod fish. Chrissy recorded them when one of the scanners in zone one pinged. Suddenly, another in zone one pinged. And then another and another.

Chrissy closed her recordings and brought up the bioscanner list. The four pings had come from scanners Q through N, backward. She was quite interested to find out what had set the four off in quick succession. She looked at the scanners' info, expecting the fish species to pop up any second. But after a few seconds, they all read "UNKNOWN SPECIES". Chrissy frowned. Were the scanners malfunctioning or had a truly unidentified species of fish really moved past all four of them?

Chrissy was about to file a report to Dan about the scanners possibly malfunctioning when scanners D through A suddenly pinged in quick succession. She watched her computer screen intently, waiting for the result. But after a few seconds, they all reported "UNKNOWN SPECIES". Chrissy blinked and her mouth dropped. That was quite unusual. She couldn't help but wonder if it was the anomaly they kept picking up, but that didn't seem to make sense as it was last recorded in zone eight, a thousand feet up and five hundred feet north.

She pulled up the seafloor map surrounding the facility. Zone one was immediately outside the facility, and as she looked at the map, looking to see where scanners A through D and N through Q were, she noticed that those eight scanners were all just outside of her sector. Scanner 1-A was just fifty feet away from her out in the briny deep. Not only that, but she noticed that the two sets of scanners were right next to each other, which meant that whatever passed by Q through N and then D through A was headed in her direction. Chrissy's heart skipped a beat—she might actually get a chance to see what their anomaly was.

Chrissy looked up at the blue viewing dome and bounced up and down on her bed. "I can't wait to see what it is!" she said to herself. Suddenly, her video caller began to ring. She sighed and answered.

"Hey, Chrissy," said Tim.

"What do you want?" she said, annoyed, as her room began to darken.

"I just want you to know that I dug up some more dirt on your hero Dr. Dorian."

"Shut up, Tim! I don't care if he drinks."

"This isn't about his alcoholism. This is about what he spends all his money on these days," said Tim with a sarcastic smile.

"Would you please piss off?!" she said as the room became darker. "I said I don't care! There's nothing you can say or do that would ruin him for me."

"Oh, I wouldn't say that."

"That's right. You *won't* say anything!" Chrissy closed her video caller before Tim could make a retort. He tried to call right back, but Chrissy slapped a 12-hour mute on his profile. She would've blocked him totally, if she could have, but the programmers who made their computers had put certain restrictions on their communications in the case of an emergency. So she would have to make do with the 12-hour mute. "Idiot."

Chrissy closed her computer and went over to her dresser. She pulled out her pajamas and began to change her clothes when suddenly the area around her dresser brightened up for a second before darkening again.

Chrissy looked around the room and finally noticed how dark it actually was. She was about to look up at the imaging dome when a spear-like shadow appeared on the floor next to her. She watched it cross her floor and disappear upon reaching the opposite wall. For whatever reason, she thought the spear shape was a fin as it was connected to the mass that now darkened her room.

Chrissy wanted to look up at the imaging dome, but every fiber of her being told her not to. Every so often, another fin-like object would show up on her floor and glide silently past. Chrissy didn't know how long her room had been darkened, but when she began to realize that it didn't seem to be ending any time soon, it began to dawn on her that something extraordinarily large was swimming above her quarters.

Chrissy swallowed hard. While shadows could look bigger than the actual animal that cast them, this shadow just kept going which implied something truly gigantic, or at the very least, extremely long.

Chrissy began to breathe fast. She closed her eyes and started bouncing on the balls of her feet. She was working herself up to look at the imaging dome. It didn't matter what the creature was, she had to see it. It was for the sake of science and it could answer so many questions.

Chrissy's breathing quickened and her heart beat faster. Finally, she clamped down on a scream and looked up, forcing her eyes open, but she saw nothing. She looked all around the imaging dome, but there was nothing outside. She then realized that at some point while her eyes were closed, the room had gotten brighter. "Dammit!" she said, throwing her shirt on the floor. "I missed it!" But then an idea struck her.

Chrissy rushed over to her computer and opened it, pulling up the video caller. She selected Richard's name and hit call. The screen rang a few times and Chrissy bounced on her bed nervously. "Come on, Richard. Come on. Please be awake."

The screen flashed and Richard's face appeared as he rubbed one of his eyes. "Chrissy," he yawned. "What's the matt—whoa," he said, seeing her in her bra and jeans. "It must be my birthday."

"Richard! Turn on your imaging dome! Now!"

"What? Why?"

"Just do it!"

"I don't think so. I don't enjoy seeing the blackening deep from the bottom."

"Please! I think whatever our anomaly is just passed by my room."

"What? Are you serious? Did you get a look at it?"

"No! I was too scared."

"Too scared? What do you mean?"

"Just turn on your dome!"

"All right, all right." Richard lifted the control and begrudgingly switched it on.

"Do you see anything?!"

"No," he said, shaking his head. "Are you sure you didn't dream this?"

"I'm sure! Bioscanners in zone one were going off like mad before it passed by here. Scanners Q through N went off, in that order, and then D through A. It took me a while to realize that whatever it was, was heading straight for me."

"Why didn't you see it?"

"I got distracted by Tim and then forgot about it."

"Distracted how?"

"Never mind! Look up! Are you sure there's nothing there?"

"I'm sure," said Richard, looking up again. "But if there is something heading my way, or if I missed it, then the scanners behind me should go off soon, right?"

Chrissy jumped. "That's right!" She pulled up the list of scanners and waited.

"Anything?" asked Richard after a minute.

"Nothing…" Chrissy's face fell. "What the hell? I don't understand."

"Well, the ocean is three-dimensional. It's possible whatever the creature was swam upward once passing your room."

"Then that means that zone five should be going off."

"And there's nothing?"

"Nothing!"

"And you didn't see anything?"

"I saw…" Chrissy's face contorted. "I saw some fin shaped shadows glide by on my bedroom floor."

"How big were they?"

"Gigantic! And they all seemed to be connected to one long mass."

"How long?"

"I don't know. A—a hundred feet? At the least. Most likely more."

"A hundred feet? Could've been a blue whale then."

"Not at twelve thousand feet below the surface!"

"All right, all right. I was just spit-balling." Richard exhaled. "Then I have no idea what it could have been."

Chrissy began to shake. The implications of the size of the creature began to well up in her mind. The only thing that kept her from cracking was the fact that it had somehow eluded all their scanners. The sheer impossibility of the situation derailed whatever madness she could've fallen into.

Richard could see that she was beginning to crack, so he said, "Listen. We can't do anything about it tonight while the team's asleep. Get some rest yourself. We'll convene in the morning and you can tell us all about it."

Chrissy nodded. "All right."

"All right. Good night."

Chrissy closed the video caller. She went back to the scanner list and none of them showed any irregularities except for the eight that had pinged before her call with Tim. How was that possible? And especially for an animal as big as this one seemed to be? True, they had all come down to the deep sea research facility to document marine life on the seafloor and possibly look for new creatures, but the possibility of finding something larger than a blue whale and at the bottom of the ocean where only the boneless horrors lived— it was too much.

Chrissy didn't sleep that night. The extremely strange animal haunted her mind and she spent the entirety of the night staring at her imaging dome, daring it to come back so she could see what it was. But a part of her truly didn't want to know.

To be continued in **The L<small>EVIATHAN</small>**

Coming 2022

Feature 2

The house on the corner was attracting a lot of attention tonight. People from all walks of life had heard about the party. Most of them were hipsters, nerds, and socialites, but the house and its party actually belonged to a different assortment of characters who were congregating in the basement. They didn't care if the collegiate elite joined them, just so long as they paid the cover charge. This different sort wore studded and spiked leather jackets and belts. They had spiky hair dyed outlandish shades of electric blue, bright pink, and safety orange. The men wore black, too tight-fitting denim trousers or professional golfer's pants while the girls settled for plaid miniskirts. Dark lipstick and eye shadow accompanied facial piercings on the girls, while men occasionally opted for chokers and a few nose piercings. Band tees were everywhere with the Sex Pistols and Ramones being well represented, while everyone else opted for the anarchist A.

They were soon joined by another punk in a studded leather jacket with a red Mohawk atop his head.

"Yo, Needles!" said another with a blue Mohawk. "You made it, man!"

"Yeah, Stud. I wouldn't miss this for the world."

"I thought you said something about your mother not wanting you to come."

"Aw, Needles' mommy didn't want him staying out late," teased a girl with green hair and a torn tank top.

"Shut up, Courtney," said Needles. "Yeah, my mother didn't want me to come, but that's because she wanted to make sure I go to church tomorrow."

"Oh, holy father, where art thou?" said Courtney with her hands clasped in a pious gesture.

"What?" said Needles.

"Isn't that what you say in church?"

"When was the last time you went to church?"

"Um…never."

"It shows."

"Isn't that just like our parents, though?" said one depressed voice from a darkened corner. "Trying to make us better people or something? It's like, I can't imagine being anything better than I am right now."

"That's a sad commentary," muttered Courtney.

"Needles, man," began Stud, "it's like this, bro—if you want to keep your mother off your case, you need to devote yourself completely to this way of life. Show her that you're never going back to the mainstream."

"I started a band," shrugged Needles.

"That's a real good start, dude. What's it called?"

"We don't have a name yet."

"You should call yourselves something like Red Piss."

"Or Black Devotion," suggested the punk from the corner.

"Or Mommy's Disappointment," suggested Courtney.

"Courtney, don't you have a line of coke to do?"

"Why does everyone keep saying that?!"

"Do you remember the last party where you kept sniffing…?"

"I was sick! Not on drugs!"

"And I suppose paranoia is a symptom of the common cold?" said Needles.

"Fever dreams! I had a fever of a hundred-and-one!"

"I've never seen anyone have hallucinations that bad."

"There's a first time for everything!"

"Dude, I got it," said Stud with a snap of his fingers. "Your mother wants you to go to church, right? Well, I say you go to church, but not your mother's kind of church."

"What do you mean?"

"Let's create an altar right here and now. We'll make our own god and worship it! And we'll consecrate it with raucous partying, dude! You in?!"

"I don't know, man… I don't believe in God to begin with, and you want me to worship a god we made up ourselves? That's even less believable than what my mother's church teaches."

"How do you know the god we create for ourselves doesn't exist?" asked Stud. "You ever heard of the Law of Attraction? Whatever you put energy into becomes real? Well, maybe it's the same for gods. You believe in them and they exist. Maybe that's how your mother's god works."

Needles cocked an eyebrow. "I don't know…"

"Come on, man! Hey, you remember that time Dave kept saying it was going to rain that one day, and we all kept telling him he was wrong. Even the weatherman was like 'Nuh-uh!' But he kept saying, 'I don't know, man. I just think it's going to rain today.' And then it did! That was freaky, right, dude?"

"Yeah, that was pretty freaky…"

"There you go, man. Law of Attraction. And I'll tell you what, since this is supposed to be your church, it will be your god. You can make it whatever you want and call it whatever you want, and we'll all help worship it. Right, dudes?" said Stud to the room.

"Yeah!" said several of the others in unison.

"Make a god with spiky horns, like a demon," suggested one of the girls.

"Nah, dude," said one of the guys. "Make it a naked lady."

"We'll call her 'Sexerosa, the goddess of getting laid'," said another, nodding his head.

Needles took a minute to ponder this. He thought it was a ridiculous idea. How could he believe in a god he made himself when he didn't believe in anything other than what he could see? As a result, he turned down the idea. The others were disappointed, but their disappointment was soon forgotten as the first case of beer was opened and a couple of doobies made the rounds.

An hour passed, during which some of the dumbest conversations on the planet took place. But when the drunken fog reached its muggiest, the conversation turned back to their made up goddess.

"Dude, God is so lame. It's like, if you want people to worship you, you gotta be cool, bro."

"Yeah, man. Jesus never smoked bowl. For such a chill dude, he never chilled, dude. Whoa! That rhymed, dude."

"I know what sort of god I'd worship—a hot chick with huge boobs!"

"Or a hot chick with a hundred boobs!"

"Or a hot chick with a hundred, huge boobs!"

"Whoa! Dude, now, you're talking, dude."

"But if it's going to be a chick," began one of the girls as she took a drag, "she should have cool hair, like us. Blue or black or orange or red."

"Something like us," added one of the girls.

"Exactly."

"She could be the goddess of punks!" said one of the guys. "The goddess of getting laid, getting high, sticking it to the man, and getting rich!"

"Fuck yeah, dude!"

"Hey, Betsy," said one of the guys, coughing from inhaling too deeply. "You're really good at art, right?"

"Yeah, man."

"You could draw our goddess for us."

Betsy took a second to process this before her blood shot eyes lit up. "Yeah, man! I can draw her! Get me some paper and colored pencils, and I'll make you a goddess worth worshipping!"

"Hell yeah!"

"Hey, man. What're those things at a church where the holy man stands behind it and lectures at you from? You know, the table thing?"

"An altar?"

"Naw, man. That's not it."

There was a pause until someone said, "Shit, dude. Do you mean an altar?"

"Yeah, man! An altar! Our church needs an altar. We can make an altar and prop our goddess on top of it."

"Yeah!" cheered several of them.

"Let's get to it, then!" said Stud.

And with that, the punks started to create their church and goddess. Someone got Betsy a notebook and an eight-pack of colored pencils, while the rest of them started to create an altar out of empty beer cases. After a few minutes, they had their shoddily thrown together altar and a quickly scribbled together goddess that barely looked anything like they had described. Despite that though, Betsy showed them her work and they all approved.

"That's kick ass, Betsy! You're one badass bitch!"

"And don't you forget it!"

They propped up the notebook against the wall on top of the altar and stood back, admiring their handy work.

"Yo, dude," one said. "Shouldn't we like, be on our knees or something, offering it sacrifices and stuff?"

"Yeah, man!" said the rest of them. So, while most of them got on their knees and began bowing before the altar, one of them put a half empty beer can, a baggie with a little weed left over, and a line of cocaine on the altar before the icon of the goddess.

"All hail…!" one said, but then stopped as they hadn't given it a name. Despite that, the rest of them started chanting, "Allhail! Allhail! Allhail!"

Suddenly, there was a click from up the stairs and everyone stopped, looking panicked with their eyes popping out of their sockets. The person that came down the stairs was Needles.

"Sorry about that, dudes. You wouldn't believe how long the line for the bathroom was."

"All right," said one of the punks. "It's Needles! Welcome to the party, dude."

"Dude, how high are you? I've been here the whole time. I just needed to take a piss, man."

"Oh…"

"What's going on here?"

"We made our own church," said Stud.

"This is our goddess," said Courtney. "Her name is Allhail."

"Allhail?"

"All hail, Allhail!" one chanted.

"All hail, Allhail! All hail, Allhail! All hail, Allhail!" they said in unison.

"She's the goddess of getting laid, getting high, sticking it to the man, and getting rich!"

"No! She's the goddess of getting high, getting laid, getting rich, and sticking it to the man!"

"What did I say, man?"

"You said she was the goddess of getting laid, getting high, sticking it to the man, and getting rich."

"Oh, my bad, man."

"Come on, Needles!" said Stud. "Get on your knees and worship your new goddess!"

Needles paused. For some reason he knew he was against this, but he couldn't remember why. He sometimes forgot stuff when he was high or drunk. He wondered if there was a way to fix that. But since he couldn't remember what his objections were, he shrugged and knelt down beside the others.

"All hail, Allhail! All hail, Allhail! All hail, Allhail!" they chanted.

"Right," said Stud, standing. "Enough of that. Let's show our goddess what sort of congregation we are and fucking party!"

"Yeah!" they cheered.

At that, the beer started flowing freely, more joints were rolled, coke appeared, and someone did the line that was left on the altar. They put an old Sex Pistols album on the turntable and cranked the volume to eleven. It didn't take long before some of them started pairing up and making out. And so, they consecrated their new church and goddess in a true punk revolt.

The night wore on and the substance abuse took its toll. The coke sniffers eventually worked themselves up into a paranoid frenzy and left the basement to flee their delusions. The potheads and drunks meanwhile collapsed and passed out wherever their butts landed. It was well past two in the morning by the time all the punks had fallen into a deep sleep.

But there was one who wasn't sleeping: Needles. He hadn't smoked or drunk as much as the others, and before midnight, he had extricated himself and joined the party upstairs where someone had supplied the house with pizza and soda. He kept a few slices and a two liter company, thinking about their new goddess Allhail. It dawned on him how she had gotten that name.

He kept thinking about what Stud had said about religion operating like the Law of Attraction—that God only worked if you had any belief in it. That may have been the reason why certain religions were always so unhappy—because they believed themselves to be in accordance with God's righteous indignation. They suffered because they believed they had to.

Needles still wasn't sure he could buy into that proposition since he was familiar with plenty of Bible stories that went against that theory. But as he smoked a cigarette over a half-eaten slice of pepperoni, he started to reconsider Stud's words. Not that he had suddenly found faith, but when he considered the future and how he would like to be a world-famous punk rock star, he didn't see God granting him his prayer as it would entail a lot of drugs, booze, and tail. But if the power of their goddess was genuine, then she would hear his prayer. And even if she didn't have any power, there would be no harm in actually trying.

His mind made up, he extinguished his cigarette in his pizza and headed for the basement. He found everyone passed out, which he was thankful for. He didn't want anyone to see what he was about to do.

He stepped over bodies as he made his way to the altar. He prostrated himself before it, and as he bent forward, he said, "Oh, goddess Allhail. I pray thee. Please grant my request. I want to be a world-famous punk rock star, but I doubt God will grant my prayer. Won't you smile upon me and give me thy blessing? Oh, all powerful goddess. Hear thy servant's plea."

Needles stayed bent over on the ground for a few seconds, but when nothing happened, he sat up. "I don't know what I expected. Oh, well," he said, standing. "No harm trying."

Needles turned to see if there was any dope still around so he could pass out himself. He had his back to the altar and didn't notice as a chilly fog began to emanate from the picture of the goddess. As he bent down to pick up a joint, he saw a mist gather around his feet. He turned around and saw the fog surrounding the makeshift altar and goddess icon. His mouth dropped and he felt a chill go down his spine, but nothing could have prepared him for what happened next.

The eyes of the icon flashed purple and locked with his own. An amorphous black cloud formed before the altar and out stepped a figure. It had pale white skin, a naked, female form, a hundred large breasts, and electric blue spiky hair. Its eyes were red with black slits and its smile made Needles want to wet his pants.

"Come," she commanded. "Come here, my servant. Kneel at my feet."

Needles moved without thinking and kneeled before her.

"Bow to me."

Needles bowed, planting his face to the floor.

"Now," said the entity, running her ice cold hand along Needles' scalp, "worship me."

"A-All hail, Allhail. All hail the goddess of getting high, getting laid, getting rich, and sticking it to the man. All hail, the goddess of punks."

"Good," she cooed. "Now, love me."

"I love thee," said Needles with a stammer.

"Adore me."

"I adore thee…"

"Forsake all other gods in favor of me," she hissed.

"I forsake all gods in favor of Allhail, the goddess of punks."

"Look into my eyes," she commanded.

Needles was nearly a gibbering mess, but he did as he was told and lifted his eyes to look into hers. When he did so, he could feel a heat unlike any other on his eyeballs. He thought for sure they were going to burst into flame.

"I have heard the prayer of my servant," she said. "You wish for fame. You wish for money. You wish for groupies."

Needles nodded.

"I can give you all that and more," she said sweetly, leaning down to him. "But not without a sacrifice."

Needles paused. "A sacrifice?"

"A sacrifice," repeated the goddess.

"What do you want?" gibbered Needles. "Beer, pot, coke?"

Allhail giggled. "No, I was birthed through your raucous festivities. I am your substance abuse made manifest. I can get high or drunk just by willing it. What I want, Needles, is something specific from you."

Needles swallowed. "Like my blood?"

"No."

"My life?"

"Getting warmer."

Needles gulped. "My soul?"

"In due time, yes! But not tonight."

Needles paused again. "My virginity…?"

The goddess paused and blinked. She then cackled with the force of a thousand ice storms. "You *wish*, little man! No, what I want is for you to desecrate a holy site in my name. I want you to offer up your faith for me by sacrificing your faith for…" Allhail's face lost its jovialness as she pointed upward. "Go to the church your mother attends, the Church of the Holy Shepherd, break in, and ransack the place. Shatter the pews, burn the hymnals, urinate on the holy icons, smash the windows, violate the tabernacle, and when you are finished, come back to me, and I will make your wildest dreams come true! Do we have a deal?!" she said.

Needles paused as sweat dripped down his face. Could he really do what she was asking? And how did he know she would keep her end of the bargain?

"How do I know you'll fulfill your end of the bargain?" he asked.

"Look here," she said. She expanded her hands as a CD cover flashed into existence. It pictured Needles' band on the front and bore the name they did not yet have, but seemed fitting: All Hail. "And look at this," she said, waving her hand, and in an instant, Needles lived a thousand moments at once. He felt the dollar bills in his hand, he could hear his bank calling him to make sure the money in his account was legitimate, he could hear the snap and see the flash of pictures being taken, he could feel people pulling him in all directions, he could feel the high of designer drugs, he felt the haze of foreign booze, and he felt the weight of women upon his lap as they stroked his genitals.

"Well?" she said, leaning forward again.

"Deal!" said Needles, taking her icy hand.

To be continued in **Tales of Horror Vol. II: Malicious Spirits**

Coming 2022

Author's Afterword

Good news, everyone!

 Thank you for reading Tales of Horror: Macabre Monsters of Michigan. I hope it thrilled and chilled you.

 TOH here is the genesis of my "Tales of" books. I don't remember how I came up with the idea originally, but I think I saw it as a convenient way of publishing short stories, which is a convenient way of building up my indie author reputation without having to rely solely on novels or the traditional means of publishing short stories. But, regardless of my reasoning, my "Tales of" series is starting to take on a life of its own. I have a Tales of Romance that I re-published earlier this year, I'm writing TOH2 and TOR2, and I have plans for a Thriller Tales, Tales of Comedy, and several dozen more volumes of TOH. I have ideas literally for years. Tales of Horror is going to be the foundation of my indie author career, which may or may not be a good thing. And it all started with a short story for a creative writing class back at Wayne State where a guy encounters a werewolf-like creature stealing his chickens. And yes, the original version was in email format. An "epistolary" the learned men call it. Just like how *Frankenstein*, *Dracula*, and most of the New Testament are written in letters and journal entries.

 Anyway, I do truly hope you enjoyed the stories contained within this anthology, and I hope you will continue to join me along my writing journey. I call myself the Omni-Genre Writer, so I should have something for everyone…eventually. And if you enjoyed this book, I would like to invite you to leave a review as that will help me find my audience and help me pay off my student loan debt. (Don't major in English, kids.) But, if you didn't like it, then I apologize. Maybe I'll make it up to you in the future.

 Follow me on Instagram at bryanclaesch or check out my website at www.bryanclaesch.com/ to keep up to date with me and everything I'm doing.

Thank you for your patronage.

BCL

About the Author

Bryan C. Laesch calls himself the Omni-Genre Writer, despite some evidence to the contrary. He writes in every genre and has written in every style…that he likes.

Born from a random assignment where he decided to write about an encounter with the legendary cryptid known as the Dogman, Bryan launched himself into the world of horror with intentions to delve deeper. Thanks to his interest in the macabre, and thinking that most horror media relies too much on cheap, jump scares, gratuitous gore, naked sluts, dumb characters, and bad writing, Bryan has taken it upon himself to write good horror stories with smart characters and actually terrifying monsters. He hopes to one day stand on equal ground with Bram Stoker, Mary Shelley, Edgar Allan Poe, HP Lovecraft, and Stephen King.

When not crafting tales that thrill and chill, he may be found blogging about MBTI, peddling t-shirts through Transcendent Tees, or pursuing one of his several dozen interests.

He currently resides in Metro Detroit, MI, but has dreams of living out in the country.

.

Contact Info:

E-Mail: bryanclaesch@yahoo.com

Website: www.bryanclaesch.com/

Facebook: htttps://www.facebook.com/thewriterbryanlaesch

Instagram: https://www.instagram.com/bryanclaesch

Twitter: https://www.twitter.com/BryanofAllTrade

Transcendent Tees Site: www.transcendenttees.store

Join Bryan's Newsletter or become a Beta Reader for him here:
https://forms.gle/YXeKf6qB5KEs7tvU8